# Someone to Care

By Carole Parker

Carole Parker

copyright © 2020 Carole Parker

All rights reserved.

ISBN:9798664123845

# DEDICATION

To three men who greatly influenced my life.

My grandfather, who showed me we are only limited by our imagination.

My father, who taught me to reach for the sky but never forget my roots.

My husband, who encouraged and supported my dreams.

# CONTENTS

Chapter One　　9

Lee

Chapter two　　35

Margaret

Chapter Three　　85

Stephen

Chapter Four　　119

Chantelle

Chapter Five　　147

Lily

About The Author　　202

New November　　203

2020

# ACKNOWLEDGMENTS

My Family and Friends in the UK and Syros, Greece for their continued support, advice, and encouragement.

To the people and organisations who work together to make everyone's life matter.

Metropolitan Police, NHS, Domestic Violence Support Groups, RADAR, Drugs and Alcohol Support Groups, Autism Awareness, Mental Health Services, Emmaus Charity, Learning Disability Services, Rehabilitation Services, Age UK, The Salvation Army, District Nurses and the many others who's daily work involves caring for others.

# Chapter One

# LEE

'Anyone can become angry, that is easy. But to be angry with the right person, to the right degree, at the right time, for the right purpose and in the right way- this is not easy.'

Aristotle

**And so, it begins…**

The room feels cold, claustrophobic, I sit waiting on a plastic chair under bright light from the fluorescent tube above. The only other items of furniture are a wooden table and another plastic chair, nothing on the walls, just pale cream emulsion, covered with dark scuff marks where people have rubbed against it. No windows. The Policewoman, Mary Smith, has invited me for an 'informal' chat at ten. It is now ten-fifteen and I wait. There is no real indication why she wants to see me, she just said there has been an incident, my name has been given as a possible witness. I had requested more details; none had been forthcoming. Of course, I could have refused to attend, however, I am not like that, I am honest, law abiding and basically nosey, I want to know what it is all about.

The door opens, PC Smith strides in, she is probably ten years younger than my daughter, tall rather skinny, her dark hair is cut short and neat. She smiles, "Sorry to keep you waiting, thank you for coming in to see me. It should not take long." She takes the seat opposite me, I feel like I am in some cheap police drama, any minute now the 'bad cop' will come in and start throwing his weight around. I nod, " OK, I am curious as to why I am here?"PC Smith nods sympathetically, "I understand. It is with regards to an incident which occurred two days ago, at."

She checks her paperwork, "45, Cherrywood Avenue, Thornton. Do you know the address?" I nod. "Before we go any further, I would like to take some details for my records. May we start by your name, date of birth and your permanent address." She has a form and pen to the ready.

"My name is Carla Saxon; I was born on third of December nineteen fifty-six. I live at Number twelve, Forest Ridge, Lower Astley." She does not look up, "Marital status and dependent children?"

I reply, "I am a widow, two children boy and a girl, both adults now and living with their partners." When she finishes writing, "Carla, I believe you work for Thornton Municipal Council, Social Services?" I nod. "Can you please confirm your job title and department."

I fidget in my seat, "I am a Support Worker, I work for the Vulnerable Adults Team." "Thank you, can you please explain to me what your job as a Support Worker entails." I mumble as I try to gather my thoughts, this is like a first job interview, except I am more nervous,

"I work with individuals and sometimes their families, who are finding it difficult to cope with everyday life. They often have difficulties with their health, emotional or relationship problems. Frequently, problems related to alcohol or drugs." She is now scribbling frantically. "So, Carla, what sort of things do you actually do?" I am a little unsure how much of this is actually needed.

"Well, we help clients to budget their money, things like paying their bills on time, we can also help with benefit claims. We assist with some domestic tasks, we help promote healthy lifestyles, things like going to the gym and eating a nutritious diet. We basically cover most living skills; the main work tends to be emotional support and advice. We work with lots of other agencies for different issue, more specialist areas, such as mental health, drug and alcohol abuse, medical and housing issues. Oh! and we do a lot of computer work, filling in forms and writing reports." I give a half laugh.

PC Smith's pen is now going to catch fire it is moving so quick. She smiles, "sounds similar to our job. Now I believe you have been working with an individual at 45, Cherrywood Avenue. Lee? he says you have worked together for about six weeks, is that correct?" I nod. "Did you ever meet the owner of the property, a Mr John Hewitt? "

I had met him a few times, but he was not very sociable, "Yes, a few times, we didn't talk much." Placing her pen down she says, "Sorry, would you like a coffee?" I answer yes, my mouth is dry, partly nerves, partly too much talking. A few moments later she returns with two plastic cups of coffee.

"Just regular I'm afraid but it is warm and wet. Did you visit Lee on 14th November 2007?" I nod, "yes, that was a Monday, right?" She indicates I am right, "That is correct. Could you tell me in as much detail as you can, what has been happening since you first began supporting Lee? I am trying to get background details. Please take your time."

**First Visit**

I am somewhat surprised when I first arrive at 45, Cherrywood Avenue. It is in a part of town I have never visited before, a tree lined avenue with individually designed detached houses. An area which says good income, two point four children, two cars, three holidays a year. Number forty-five is hidden behind a privet edge, the garden looks overgrown, though the shrubs and roses suggest it has once been well cared for. It is a 'mock-Tudor' style, with a black and white facade a leaded windows, the wooden front door has an old-fashioned knocker, is set inside a porch. I knock.

Lee had been a client of social services for many years, the records show he left the area two years ago, following a dispute with neighbours. The neighbour's garden shed had caught fire, they said it had been started deliberately by Lee, he denied it. There had been protests, police and fire services were involved. Following a general demand by residents of the estate to move Lee, an eviction notice was issued by the council. Lee is classified as 'vulnerable,' so the council secured a place for him to live, in the neighbouring village. No longer under Thornton Social Services.

Now Lee is back, a fresh referral has been made by the district nurses, who have been attending the property. Lee decided to deny the nurses access, stating they were no longer needed. The nurses were actually there to see the owner of the property, a Mr John Hewitt. Lee's aggressive attitude had raised their concern,

When I read Lee's file it is a catalogue of disputes, he has been forcibly evicted by the council on three occasions, each time disputes with neighbours. Major, his large dog, of mixed breed, was involved in the incidents and was reported as aggressive. The notes state that the dog has never actually attacked anyone. However, the neighbours complained the dog was extremely noisy, barking most of the day and night. The RSPCA had been summoned, they found the dog to be in good condition, well fed with adequate space for his exercise needs. Lee kept the dog indoors at night, he also demonstrated full control over Major. The Officer's report could see no reason for removal of the dog, who was clearly devoted to its owner.

I knock again. The risk assessment states that before I enter, I must ask Lee to put the dog either outside in the back garden, or in the kitchen. Lee opens the door, he is holding Major by the collar, the dog is pulling to break free. I step back. "Hello Lee? I am Carla from Social Services, would you please put the dog in the back garden."Lee looks at me, assessing whether or not to obey, "I'll have to lock him in the kitchen, someone broke the fence down last night." With that he shuts the door. I can hear the dog barking and another male voice inside.

A few moments later Lee returns, I follow him into the sitting room. The settee had been used as a bed, a quilt and pillow at one end. The room is dark due to the leaded windows and heavy fabric curtains. The furniture is good quality oak, probably thirty years old, dark with a thin layer of dust. Lee suggests we go into the dining room, which is next to the kitchen, when Major hears our voices he begins to bark. Lee shouts, "Major down, down." There is instant quiet. "Good dog," I comment. Lee watches me,
"So why are you here?" I explain the reason for my visit, "It is because the district nurses are worried, apparently you would not let them in? They needed to give treatment to the man who lives here." Lee rolls both eyes to the ceiling,

"John does not want those nosey busy bodies coming around, he is fine." I have read a little about John, so I try to reason, "John is seventy-seven years old, he needs help, medical help to change his dressing. He also suffers difficulties with his breathing. The meals which were delivered, I understand you cancelled them too?" Lee is now pulling at a thread on the tablecloth. He is dressed in jeans and sweater, with workman style boots, I see a black leather jacket hung on the door. His arms are covered in tattoos, Lee replies,

"John is old, not stupid. He has a small ulcer on his right shin, I make sure it is kept clean. I also shop, cook and clean for John, in return he lets me stay here." I decide not to get into a confrontation at this stage.

"Oh, very good, a mutually convenient arrangement. Do you stay on the sofa, I noticed it was made up as a bed? "Lee stares defiantly at me, "No, I sleep upstairs. John prefers to sleep down, he goes to bed late, watches TV a lot. There is a toilet down here too." I am seeking a safe subject for conversation. "Where did you meet John?"Lee stands up, now towering over me, "At the bloody pub, what has that got to do with anything, are you like them other nosey, busy bodies?"

I sit quietly for a few moments; Lee obviously has a short fuse. "Have you had the dog a long time? He is really nice, what is his name?" Lee is obviously wondering if this is some kind of trick question. "Five years, his name is Major. He is a good dog, loyal, obedient, he could do better than any of them so called pedigree dogs, he is clever." Lee is more comfortable talking dogs. "I agree with you, mixed breed dogs are often loyal and clever. I had one from the dog rescue shelter, mixture of terrier and other breeds, definitely a Heinz Variety. Does John get along with Major?" I ask."Yeah, though he plays too rough with him, he is a big dog, I train him not to jump up. Unless he has the attack command, then he really goes for it. John doesn't understand, Major gets over excited when he teases him."

I ask, "Is John at home now?" Lee nods, "Yeah he is upstairs reading, doesn't like company." I smile, "That 's OK. It was you I came to see. Are you alright for money? Did you get some benefits sorted?" Lee looks coyly and asks, "Why?" I reply immediately, "If you haven't got your benefits, I can help you. I can also help getting you a bus pass. I know that you have just moved back here, do you remember you had support when you lived here before?"Lee nods,

"Yeah that was OK, got me a free gym membership too. I have had a letter from the benefits, they are asking questions about rent and stuff, I have not been back to see them yet. You could help me to sort that. I need to get a bank account too."At last I am finding a way to start working with Lee, "OK, how about Wednesday morning we could meet up and go to the bank and the Benefits Office, I will try and make an appointment. I will also find out about local gyms if you are interested."Lee grins "OK, can we make it about eleven because I have to get John's breakfast first." I nod agreement.

There is one more thing I have to ask. "Lee do you know if John has any children?" Lee moves towards the kitchen door, "Yes, he has a son, real nasty piece of work, I sent him away the other day, he was shouting and swearing at me. John was not home, John told me if Malcolm ever comes round, do not let the grabbing bastard in. Major and me saw him off. He is always phoning and arguing with John, he does not like me." I look at Lee sympathetically. Although, I can understand how a family member would be deeply concerned, to discover a complete stranger has moved in with an elderly relative. Not to mention, with a large, aggressive dog. We chat for another thirty minutes, mostly about dogs, Lee is an expert on canine care, diet, and training. Eventually we say goodbye, with the understanding that we will meet outside the bank at eleven on Wednesday

When I get back to the car, I can smell nicotine on my clothes, although Lee did not smoke, the ashtrays had cigarette ends in and there was a packet of Marlborough and a lighter on the coffee table. Lee is an odd young man, he has almost feminine features, his head is shaved, except for a longer strip of hair down the centre. He is incredibly skinny, he wore a shirt, buttons opened to halfway down his hairless chest. I wonder if he has been eating proper food, I did not gain access to the kitchen, maybe next time. I would also liked to have met John, however, gently, gently, I needed to build up trust.

**Second Visit**

I meet Lee on Wednesday outside the bank, unfortunately he has brought the dog. He ties Major up outside and we go in. Lee does not have enough information to open a bank account, we come away with a list of things he needs to take in, including his Passport or some other formal identification. Outside the bank there are six youths waiting near the dog, they appear to be teasing Major. They obviously know Lee, one of them calls his name.

Lee becomes overly aggressive; he unties the dog and holding Major's lead, he raises his voice, "Piss Off", encouraging the dog to bark. One of the youth's shouts, "That dog should be muzzled it's fucking wild, like you, you are a real fucking headcase." The youths start shouting abuse, Lee holds the lead and shouts, "Attack." Major is on his hind legs, barking, froth around his mouth. I am sure if it breaks free, he will kill or severely maim the boys. They move back, they are still shouting abuse, but I see they are scared of the dog. By now a small crowd has gathered across the street, it is all pretty scary and embarrassing.

After the incident, Lee refuses to accept any further

support today, the trip to the benefits office is postponed. I suggest that Major might be better left at home next time. I walk part of the way back with Lee, I have a dread the youths might return. Lee seems confident he can look after himself, I wonder how confident he would be without Major.

**Third Visit**

The following Monday, Lee appears anxious as he opens the door. I am introduced to John Hewitt, the gentleman who owns the house. John is extremely thin, his eyes are sunken into his skull, he has a red, bulbous nose which is usually associated with heavy drinkers. He is wearing pyjamas and dressing gown. "Good Morning, John. I am Carla from Social Services." He smiles wanly, "You here to help Lee, he needs to get a job, give him some purpose." Lee comments, "I told you John, she is going to help me get a bank account and sort out my benefits, until I can get a job. Now do you want cereal?"

John shakes his head, "just a cup of tea for me." Lee strides off to the kitchen, calling out, "I will make you some toast, you need to eat."

John looks to me, "worse than being married, he can really nag." I smile, watching as John lights a cigarette and immediately begins coughing, a deep, chesty smokers cough. I wait till the coughing stops.

"How long have you lived here John?" he gives a little laugh, "Too bloody long, must be fifty years now, lost my wife two years ago, damn cancer got her. Bless her, It won't be long now till I am joining her." I decide to be more positive, "I understand you are receiving help from the district nurses, how has that been?" John flicks his ash into the ashtray, he has not actually smoked any of the cigarette as yet.

"Yeah, they nag me about my smoking but apart from that fine, they change the dressing on my leg, ulcers will not heal." John raises his pyjama pants to show me the dressing. "They didn't show last week so Lee cleaned and dressed my leg, he's a good lad."

Lee returns with a tray of tea, toast, and a glass of water. Next to the water is an egg cup containing tablets and an inhaler. John picks up the egg cup, "Have to take the pills, it's a wonder I don't rattle. What's this pink one for Lee?" Lee leans over, "you have warfarin to thin your blood, a heart tablet for your blood pressure, a steroid for your breathing, a calcium tablet and a happy pill which is pink." John shakes the contents into his hand and swallows them all, except the large calcium tablet, which he chews.

We visit the Benefits Office. Lee soon becomes impatient with the questions and is on the point of walking out when asked, "So why have you never worked Lee?" The woman watches Lee, he stands up and walks to the door, I quickly follow him. "Lee wait, it is a fair question." Lee spins around,
"What am I supposed to say, I spent half my life drugged up in isolation wards? I am trying to get my act together, they just judge me from their ivory tower, they haven't got a clue." I can see how difficult this is for him, "Lee, please come back, let me speak to her." The woman has been watching from behind her screen. This is one of the first branches in England to introduce safety screens between advisors and clients, it is a little unnerving. "Lee has a condition, Autism; he finds it difficult to secure employment. We can obtain a letter from his doctor if required. In the meantime, Lee has nothing to live on, no family to help."

The woman regards me suspiciously, "we will require evidence, it may be that Lee is entitled to some form of disability payment." Lee is staring at the floor. I nod, Lee is wringing his hands, his body is trembling. I decide it is better for us to leave now.

"Thank you for your help, we will be in touch." I say, as I steer Lee towards the door.

Outside Lee is like a bottle of lemonade, which has been shaken, ready to burst forth and spray anyone in sight, I guide him across the road to the park. We walk quietly for ten minutes. I can see he is becoming calmer. "Don't worry Lee, I will sort this out." I am not sure how, but I believe he should be on a disability benefit. I have read his file, he is Autistic, he is extremely anxious, when he feels swamped by multiple tasks or sensory stimulation, his anxiety bubbles over as anger. There are methods for managing, coping with these symptoms, however, Lee's chaotic background has meant little stability or support work to help him develop strategies.

PC Smith stops writing, "thank you Carla, you have been highly informative. Unfortunately, I have another interview in five minutes, I wonder if we might continue with your information tomorrow? Would nine o'clock be alright for you? Or maybe earlier?" I am an early riser, so we finally agree on eight o'clock the next day. I am still curious,

"Do you mind if I ask, has something happened to Lee?" She collates her papers, "No. Mr Hewitt was found dead at his home last Monday evening, his son Malcolm found him. We are investigating the death; Mr Hewitt junior has made a number of complaints which we are following up. Lee is presently helping us with our inquiries." I am shocked, that poor man, I knew he was not too well, but I never suspected he would die, Lee must be devastated. What did she mean 'helping us with our inquiries?' What sort of 'complaints' has Malcolm made? PC Smith declined to give me any further information at this stage.

Back at the office, it is a busy day, everyone, is coming or going, computers are all taken, and someone has used up all the milk! I offer to go and buy some and pick up a sandwich in the process. I inform Bill, my manager, about the police interview; he is very understanding and says he will arrange cover for me the following morning. I am concerned about Lee, his anxiety levels will have reached an all-time high, I decide to ask if I can see him tomorrow.

I have another call in half an hour, Lacey, a linked social worker, is picking me up. We are off to see a new client who suffers from agoraphobia, she has apparently not left her house for two years. Lacey arrives ten minutes later. Today she is wearing a pair of trousers, which are cut wide to resemble a skirt. They are purple with motifs of flowers and trees, stitched on at random intervals. A sort of walking fairy-tale forest. Her top is also purple but a lighter shade, with bell shaped sleeves, in a soft flowing material. Lacey's size means whatever she wears, there is a lot of material, she is a large lady and proud of it. Lacey has her hair swept back into a short ponytail.
"I will just have this then we can leave, she takes out half a French stick of bread, which is oozing various items of salad, ham and cheese. Alan arrives, smiles as he spots Lacey, "Good afternoon, when I reach your age, I too will wear purple." He laughs at his own joke. Lacey grins,
"Cheeky sod, you will never see that time of life again, thermals

and bed socks for you!" She pushes the last of her sandwich into her mouth and stands to leave. I gather my jacket and bag. Lacey is driving, I am pleasantly surprised to find her car is clean inside and out, I see now it is a navy blue mini, not a black one. There are no discarded sweet papers or empty sandwich containers on the rear seat.

"Car's looking great Lacey, when did you get it done?" she grins and squeezes into the front seat, "Yesterday, that place in town, cost me forty pounds but it was worth it."

We arrive at the client's address, it is an average semi, on an average road. All driveways and grass frontage neatly matching. Lacey explains. "This referral came via her GP, her name is Janet Meredith, she lives here with her husband and three teenage children. Janet became unwell two years ago, depression and anxiety. She does not go out; she finds it difficult to be around people. Her family are concerned that her anxiety levels are increasing, she is fearful of stepping outside the front door."

Lacey rings the doorbell. Janet answers,

"Hello, please come in. I have been waiting for you." We follow her into an open plan lounge where she offers us a seat. Janet sits on the armchair. I notice that she is extremely anxious, her hands are writhing continually, she is now sitting on them to stop the movement. Her eyes are focused on the floor, as if fearful of seeing us. She is dressed casually in a denim skirt and blouse. Janet has soft features, a face warmed by her smile. Her hair is shoulder length, black and glossy, with a hint of curl. She looks at Lacey,

"I am Janet, I think my Doctor may have spoken to you, regarding my condition?" Lacey then introduces us, complete with job roles, she asks her how she is feeling today.

"Very anxious, I don't know what to expect. I told my doctor; I do not see what anyone can do. It is all in my head, it is my personal battle."

Lacey asks, "When did your anxiety start?" Janet stares upward, "well, it was about two years ago, I was made redundant, I had worked there since I left school." Lacey asks, "what was your job Janet?" Janet starts twisting her hands together, "I was a school secretary, I loved my job. Though it could be challenging at times. It was not just the redundancy, my Mother died a few days after I finished working, she had been very poorly, arthritis and kidney problems. Then my youngest son, well he got in trouble with the police, 'joy riding' they call it, it did not bring me any joy. It caused a lot of arguments. My husband Geoff, he fell off a ladder at work in the same month, he damaged his back, he has only recently been able to return to work. I suppose that is why I went to the doctors; I want to get back to normal." Janet stands up "Can I offer you two ladies a warm drink, tea, coffee, cocoa or hot chocolate?" We both smile and nod in unison; I opt for tea and of course Lacey asks for chocolate.

Janet returns with a tray of drinks and a plate of cake, strawberry gateaux, Lacey grins "Oh, my favourite, did you make this?" She replies, "yes I made it for today, I like to bake. Geoff and the children, well they are teenagers now, Melanie is twenty next week, they all complain they are putting weight on. They want me to work so I stop baking." She passes Lacey a large portion. I ask for just a little piece.

I prompt Janet, "Do you take any medication for your anxiety?" She nods, "Anti-depressants, I do not like taking them, I know they help. Sometimes they make me feel as though I am in a big bubble. The other week the entire family thought I was going completely crazy, really! I was in the utility room when suddenly, out of the corner of my eye, I saw something move near the washer. I panicked, ran out and locked the door, leaving whatever it was in there. When Geoff came home, I insisted he did a thorough search. He moved everything, found nothing. The next day I saw something orange disappear behind the washer, I phone Geoff at work, he came home, moved the cat bowls, pulled out the washer. Nothing. I saw glimpses of it three more times, no one believed me, my son said I needed to 'take more water with whatever I was drinking.' It became a family joke, 'any funny orange or purple creatures today mum', Geoff even suggested an appointment at the doctors, in case my tablets were causing hallucinations. This went on for ten days.

Then Trudy my friend next door popped in for coffee, as we chatted, she casually mentions, "Our Simon has been very upset, he lost Monty, we searched high and low for him.""Monty?" I ask her "yes, his pet corn snake, you would think we could see him, he is bright orange!" That evening Geoff and Mike our neighbour, investigated, they found him in the attic by the water tank, he had been coming down a small hole where the water pipe feeds the washing machine, eating the cat food. They said he had grown quite a bit. Everyone had a good laugh; I was relieved to find I was not going insane! Sorry I talk a lot when I am nervous."

Lacey and I are laughing, "Wow it is a good thing they found it, how big do those things grow to?"I ask. "Up to about six feet in length, I think, even I would have seen it by then!" Janet laughs We chuckle together and explore how it could have got into their attic. Lacey explains how we can support her, the first step will be to build her confidence. We agree a time and date, part of me hopes that Janet is allocated to me, I feel this lady could be a lot of fun to work with.

That evening I relay Janet's story of the snake to my partner Paul and we both laugh, "just imagine how she felt, she must have been doubting her own sanity, I mean you don't expect to find a snake in your kitchen , not here anyway."
Paul tells me his parents are coming over from Ireland next week, they are staying in a hotel. They will stay three days in London and three days in the North, to see Paul.

"How do you feel about meeting them?" Paul asks. "Though my mother will probably insist on asking all kinds of personal questions, she can be a little direct." I am pleased he has asked me, "That will be lovely, maybe we can take them for a meal? That new Turkish place in town?" Paul is shaking his head, "Mother does not eat anything spicy or with garlic, my Father is OK. Maybe some pub grub will be best."We spend the evening talking riddles, telling funny stories, generally acting like two silly teenagers.

### At the Station

I arrive just before eight, the desk Sergeant leads me through to the interview room and threatens me with a cup of their unrecognisable coffee. I accept. PC Mary Smith arrives on the dot of eight, "Ah, you have coffee, just a second while I get one." We exchange pleasantries about the weather, the fact that there is a Bank Holiday in a couple of weeks, as she sorts out her papers. "Now, if you can continue where we left off, I think you had been sorting Lee's benefits." I smile, "Yes I actually arranged for Lee to meet with the disability advisor, Lee can get some assistance, he is fully mobile, however, his autism restricts his movements. He struggles with transport, crowds, shopping malls, train stations, wherever the lights and sounds are amplified. We actually have an Autism team in Social Services, I made a referral for him, just waiting their reply." She nods, "please continue

**Fourth Visit**

When I arrive on the following Monday, I am surprised to see the front window has been boarded over. Something rarely seen in this area. I step out of the car and I hear someone calling, the lady from the house opposite is on her way over, "Excuse me, are you something to do with the council?"

"Yes, why is there a problem? "I reply. The woman in her mid-forties is keen to unburden her concerns. "It is that young man who has moved into John's house, there has been nothing but trouble since he arrived. We have had a terrible weekend, his sort attract trouble, I knew as soon as I saw him. He is so rude, I tried speaking to him, he just looked straight through me."

I am starting to get impatient with this lady. "So, what has he done?" Her voice is now at a high pitch,

"All weekend, from late Friday night, gangs of young men loitering around, smoking and swearing, it has been awful. Of course, we telephoned the police, when my husband saw two of them sitting on the bonnet of Margo's car. Cheeky little monkeys, I told him, 'don't you say anything to those yobs, it is not safe.' The police did not do much, just moved them along." The neighbour pulls her shirt down over her leggings, "It is him they want, the lad in John Hewitt's house. What is he doing there? He is not a relative, is he? Anyway, they were back again on Saturday evening, just after dark, they were ringing the doorbell and shouting in John's garden."

I ask if she contacted the police again, she replies, "what is the point they move them on, then as soon as the police go, they are back. Pointless. They need locking up, little Monsters. It is John I worry about; he has not been a well man you know. The police spoke to him. All this stress cannot be good for him." I nod my head.

"The window when was that broken?" I ask. She shifts uncomfortably, "last evening. The young lad came to the door with his dog, there was a lot of shouting, the dog was making a terrible racket, vicious looking thing that dog. Well, one of them threw a rock through the window. Someone must have called the police; suddenly they were here, they chased the little hooligans away. I hope they caught them. Poor John." I thank the lady and make a quick exit to the house.

Lee answers the door, he is dressed tidily, in a long-sleeved shirt and black jeans. "Hello, how are things?" I ask, Lee indicates for me to come in. "We have had a few problems. Those dickheads, the lads at the bank, you remember, well they have been here, harassing me. I wanted to set the dog on them, but John said no." John is sitting on the sofa, he has a glass in his hand which looks like whiskey, it is only ten- thirty.

"I am sorry to hear that, did the police recognise them?" John starts to cough, "They think they know the ringleader, he is from the other side of town, why go to all this trouble to harass the poor lad? It is unbelievable." John says between coughs. Lee looks sad, it is almost as though trouble follows him. He insists John eats his breakfast, of boiled egg and toast, before we leave. "He is a good carer, maybe this is what he should be looking to do as a job." I suggest. John produces a bottle of whiskey from the side of the sofa, "Hair of the dog." He grins. "What with my son Malcolm around here on Saturday shouting the odds, then that bunch of yobs, poor Lee has had a right time of it, my ticker's not doing so good either." John pours himself another drink. "Malcolm hates Lee, he will not even speak to him. I try explaining to him, he is determined, convinced that Lee is after my money. Not that I have any, this house is all I have and my pension."

I am thinking how frightening it must have been for both John and Lee, the youths, the noise, threats, Malcolm, and the police.

Later, I take Lee to meet the disability officer, she is far more understanding, she talks to him and explains what he is entitled to. She also tells him about a local group which is organised for people with autism, mostly around his age, they meet every Friday evening, play games, snooker, table tennis and have coffee, just an opportunity to chill out. Lee looks interested. It is a successful visit.

**Fifth Visit**

When I arrive today, we go into the kitchen, John is asleep on the sofa and the dog has been tied up in the garden Lee explains, "John did not sleep well, he was coughing most of the night, I wanted to call the ambulance, but he said no. He did not really settle until around four o'clock this morning. I want him to sleep now. At least when he is asleep, he is not drinking or smoking." I watch Lee as he quietly washes some dishes.

"No visits from the youths this week?" I ask. Lee shakes his head. "We've not heard anything; I went and did some shopping but there was no one around. John had a long talk with Malcolm, I think maybe they have patched things up. He is Johns only son you know. Shame not to be friends." Lee looks out of the window at Major, I think he has a gentle side hidden away.

Lee makes us both a coffee, then asks," is it OK if we stay here today, just in case John needs anything?" I assure Lee this is fine. We chat for just under an hour.

Lee grew up in the care system, he is unaware who his parents are, he was placed for adoption at birth. He had several medical issues as a child, he was born with Fetal Alcohol Syndrome, his physical development was impaired, he also had difficulties with his sight and hearing. The medical is were probably the reason he was never adopted. He did not receive an Autism diagnosis until he was twelve years old. He spent two years in a residential children's home when his foster carers struggled to manage his behaviour.

Lee speaks openly about his childhood. "It was not that bad, Julie and Tim were great, they were older, their kids had grown up and left. I liked it there, they were how I imagine grandparents. I stayed with them until I was ten." We talk about his interests, he is a keen follower of snooker, he also likes to draw. John starts to cough; Lee jumps up and goes to him. John is sitting up. Lee gets a glass of water. I think John looks poorly he smiles at me.

" It is alright dear, do not look so worried, I am always worse in a morning, true that, isn't it Lee? Maybe I will have a cup of tea now lad." His coughing stops.

Lee returns to the kitchen then suddenly shouts, "No, No Major." I go into the kitchen to see Lee outside clambering over the fence, Major has gone. After a few minutes Lee returns, he is distraught, crying, sobbing, "I can't see him, I am going to the park he might be there." I cannot let him go alone, "Wait Lee, we can go in my car, get Major's lead." I drive around the estate, we look in the gardens, every so often I stop and Lee calls Major, "He will come if he hears me, he must be scared."

The park backs onto the estate, it is where Lee walks Major every evening. After half an hour, it is beginning to feel like we are looking for a needle in a haystack, Major could be anywhere.

"Please stop the car." Lee asks. He gets out and stands in the middle of some spare ground, he shouts, "Major, Major." Nothing, we drive through the park, back around the estate to the house.

Lee is silent, he is staring trance-like. John is in the kitchen, he opens the door, he has Major on a lead. John explains, "he came back about five minutes after you left, didn't you boy," he ruffles Majors fur, Lee is on his knees hugging Major.

John continues, "Tell you what though, I reckon his rope has been cut deliberately, there is a pile of bones out there. Whoever let him free tried to distract him with food. Well, they got a surprise, because he obviously chased them off. Then he came back, to finish the bones. Reckon someone has had the fear of God put into them!!" John was laughing. I was as relieved to see Major safe; he was obviously enjoying all the attention.

"Probably best not to put Major out in the garden Lee, until the fence is fixed. I will leave you both to calm down and see you next week."

I contemplate why would anyone release Major? He had not been barking or being a nuisance, whoever he had chased probably got a bite for their trouble, though Lee had stated Major never bites unless commanded. It was a worrying development though; they could just as easily have poisoned the dog.

**Sixth Visit**

Monday morning, I arrive at the house, John opens the door, he is in his dressing gown, I realise I have never seen him dressed. "Lee has just nipped out to the local shop to get me some bread and a drop of Whiskey for later. Can I offer you a cup of tea?" He asks. I decline, he appears in good spirits, "How are you feeling today John?" I ask. "Oh, I am alright. Damn cough gets me down but there is nothing I can do about it. Lee has been fussing over me like a mother hen. I have told him, this afternoon he needs to get out, go for a walk, have a break, stuck in with an old man all the time, it is not good for him." He smiles. I realise it is hard for Lee, he has no friends, no family, nowhere to go. The door swings open and in comes Lee with Major, the dog pulls towards John, he makes a fuss of the dog, Major responds by jumping up, Lee pulls him off, but John's arms are scratched in the process. Lee is firm with the dog "Down, Major." He takes him to the kitchen. I look at John's arms, the scratches have just broken the skin. Lee says, "I will get some antiseptic and clean them." Which he gently does, despite John's protests.

Lee tells me, when we are finished, he is going to take Major out. He plans to go to the local country park, about two miles from the house, he explains the dog needs a long walk. After we have chatted for a while, I give Lee information regarding his disability claim and help him understand the forms, I complete most of the information required. The forms now need to be given to Lee's GP, fortunately he is still registered with the same doctor. I offer to drop them in on the way back to the office. John is sat on the sofa, with a glass of whiskey watching the racing as I leave.

PC Smith looks up from her copious notes, "What time did you leave?" I think for a moment, "Must have been around eleven forty-five, I remember thinking I needed to get a skate on to be at Fenwick Street by twelve." She continues writing, then says, "Thank you so much you have been very helpful."
I ask if I will be able to see Lee, she says it is not possible at the moment, but he is safe. He will be accompanied by support staff when the Police formally interview him. I am not sure how these things work; I am sure that Lee will be extremely anxious and upset about John. I explain this to PC Smith, she is very

understanding but it is out of her hands. She does, however, promise to let me know when I am able to see Lee. She suggests I might like to investigate some temporary accommodation, for when he is released.

That evening Lee consumes my thoughts. I wonder how he is coping with the loss. Death is difficult for anyone to deal with, the finality of it. Lee being on the autistic spectrum, may have difficulties. Death means change and loss, both enormous issues for him. If this is, as I suspect, Lee's first encounter with death, he will have several emotions tugging at him, he will be struggling to make sense of the loss and related sadness. Many on the autistic spectrum show emotions in a way which people not on the spectrum struggle to recognise. Their sadness may be shown in anger, laughter, silence, or tears.

I remember my first encounter with death, it happened when I was five years old. I was a pupil at St Jude's Infant School. The headmaster sent for me; I knew it was important because I had never been in his office before. Mrs Jones came with me. Mr Wood was a kind man, he always said nice things when he spoke in assembly, he made us laugh with his silly jokes. Today Mr Wood was serious.

"Carla, I have a special job for you. I want you to listen very carefully and do exactly as I say. You are friends with Yvonne in your class, do you know where she lives?" I nod my head, I have been to Yvonne's house many times, she lives over the Newsagents, her daddy owns the shop. She has the most amazing dolls house, with lights that actually work. He bends down and looks into my eyes, "You must not say anything to Yvonne, you must just go with her to the house. Her mummy died this morning. You must not tell her; Yvonne's daddy wants to tell her." I am stunned, I have never been asked to do anything so important before. I suddenly feel grown-up, responsible, I must do this for Mr Wood, for Yvonne. He asks me again if I understand, I say yes. Mrs Jones goes to get Yvonne, then the two of us set off for the two-minute walk to her house, yet this time it seems like miles. Yvonne does not ask me anything, she is unnervingly quiet. I desperately want to hold Yvonne, to tell her how sorry I am, instead I talk about her dolls house and ask if I can come and see it again. I look at her eyes, they are blank, the water in my eyes is in danger of overflowing, I talk about Mr Wood and what a funny man he is. We climb the steep stairs to her front door, Yvonne knocks. Her daddy opens the door, I can see he is crying, I have never seen a grown-up cry before, it makes me feel incredibly sad. He pulls Yvonne towards him, then nods to me and closes the door.

For a few moments I stand there, my work is done. How sad it must be in their house today. I am so glad my mummy has not died. I never got to see Yvonne's dolls house again, I never saw Yvonne. My grandmother told me her daddy sold the shop and moved miles away. I missed her.

I never met with death again until I was fifteen years old, my grandmother died. I heard the news from my mother. She had been unwell for a long time, heart problems. Everyone said she had refused to go into hospital, because the hospital building was once the workhouse, my grandmother had a fear and dread of the workhouse. She often spoke about it saying, it was a horrid place of shame, where poor people were sent, to work hard in awful conditions.

Now she was gone. I was numb, I did not really feel anything except anger, I was angry that the last time I saw her we had argued, a really bitter argument. Now I could never make that right. I could not tell her I loved her, I would miss her, how grateful I was for everything she did for me. I could not chat to her, watch her bake, listen to the banter between her and my grandfather. Then came the funeral, there were only a few people there, it felt surreal, I did not associate what was happening with my grandmother, it was all new, different people, in a strange place. Back at my parent's house people came, they were all chattering, eating sandwiches drinking cups of tea and laughing. I sat on the stairs and listened, why were they laughing? This was sad, my grandmother was dead, gone, never coming back. That was not something to laugh about. I cried for her, I cried for me and I cried at all the people who did not understand that my grandmother was a special person, who I would never see again. I dreamed a lot about my grandmother after that day, she was there in front of me, still alive. I could not go to her, touch her, talk to her, when I did, she just faded away.

I feel that Lee and John had a special relationship, an understanding, each meeting a need for the other. John wanted to help Lee. Lee needed to have someone to care for. Autism does not mean people cannot enjoy good, fulfilling relationships. Sometimes, they find it difficult to express their needs, their emotions become overwhelming, spilling into anger. I wonder how Lee is coping, do they have him in a cell? Will he be frightened?

**Police Intervention**

Paul and I drive to work together this morning, we are excited, we are planning to book a holiday at lunchtime. Some may think it is a little premature, but we have decided to go ahead. If we can bear each other's company for a full week, twenty-four-seven, then maybe we have something special. We are both agreed on the Greek islands.

At work I go into Bill's office straight away, I need him to find out what is happening to Lee, where he is. I still feel concerned, I am hoping the police have obtained specialist help for him. Bill agrees to speak to a friend on the CID team, though he cannot promise anything. "If this turns into a murder inquiry, we will probably learn nothing until it goes to court." All we learn is that the police are treating this as a suspicious death, investigations are underway. Lee is in a secure unit, not like a prison, he is being fully supported by specialist staff. Lee and I may be called as witnesses. Although the police have confirmed, neither Lee nor myself, were present at the time of death. It was Lee who found John and phoned for the ambulance, John was pronounced dead when they arrived.

It is almost two months before we hear any details of the court outcome. The inquest found that John died of a heart attack, probably induced by alcohol and cigarettes. There were scratches on his arms which had been caused by the dog. The police found the dog to be aggressive and out of control, it had been put to sleep. Lee made a video statement for the court; he was not well enough to attend. John had bruises in the form of hand-prints at the top of each arm, suggesting John had been shaken violently, the bruises had been made around the same time as his death. The police had captured the youth who smashed John's window, he gave the police the names of the other five youths, one of the youths was Michael Hewitt, Malcolm's son. John's grandson.

The youths were cautioned and ordered to attend anti bullying sessions, the one who smashed the window was made to pay the damages. All the boys were under the age of sixteen.

Malcolm had been interviewed and admitted he was with his Father on the afternoon of his death, a neighbour had seen him leaving the house. He admitted they had argued, during the interview he broke down and said he had physically shaken his Father, trying to make him see sense. Malcolm swore his Father was still alive when he left. The Judge commented that this action could have been contributory to John's death. However, his health and lifestyle were significant factors. No charges were made against Malcolm.

Lee is currently receiving treatment, medication and anger management therapy in a psychiatric hospital. He is now reported to be making good progress. Lee lost his two best friends, John and Major. He lost his home. I feel for Lee, his life has been a constant struggle, trying to make sense of the world, his feelings and emotions. I sincerely hope his future is brighter and the world is more tolerant towards Lee and people like him.

Sometimes we have cases like this, people come into the system, they engage with the service, we try to improve things for them. Then for whatever reason, they are gone. Frequently, we never hear from then again.

# Chapter Two

# MARGARET

'Success is failure turned inside out,
the silver tint of the cloud of doubt,
And you never can tell how close you are,
it may be near when it seems so far,
So, stick to the fight when you are hardest hit,
It's when things seem worst that you must not Quit.'

Author Unknown

**Margaret's Story**.

Margaret and David Unwin were married in a church. Both families attended it was a perfect day, even the weather had blessed them. Margaret wore white, her long dark hair fell in soft curls over her shoulders, a simple tiara, and a small bouquet of yellow roses added to the elegance. The groom wore a traditional suit with tails, grey; a single yellow rose adorned his buttonhole. They were a perfect couple. After only a year David had proposed, Margaret had accepted without hesitation. Everyone knew David was madly in love with her, he doted on her. It was the little things that made it special, his attention to detail, he always tried to make everything perfect. Little notes and cards with loving messages given randomly, sometimes he would surprise her, arriving outside work with a bunch of flowers or chocolates, or arrive early, unannounced with wine and a takeaway. David was a provider, he worked hard and managed everything with military precision, his life was regimented and orderly, he was dependable.

When Margaret looked back, the first few months were idyllic, she could not remember the exact day or week when things started to change. Maybe things had not changed, maybe love truly was blind. Psychological abuse, that is what the textbooks called it. Margaret studied psychology, her degree was obtained from Sheffield University, she knew about these things. It could never happen to her. Her dream had been to be a child psychologist. That was her career when she met David, he was a technical director with a computer firm. As Margaret reflected on those days, his quirky little ways now appeared odd, more demanding. Towels had to be hung a particular way, toothbrushes placed in holders, with a cover to protect the bristles. Tins always stacked with labels facing forward, no crumbs to be left on the breadboard. There was an endless list of David's specifications. If any of his specifications were not met, he would sulk, sometimes for hours. Then he would repeatedly raise the errors in conversation.

At first Margaret had challenged his attitude, this made him angry, he would shout and slam doors. She recalled when he smashed their wedding photograph, because she had forgotten to buy his special soya milk. For two days they argued. Then he came home with a silver necklace, apologised and begged forgiveness for his temper. He was so loving, so sorry and that night they made love more intensely than ever before. That was the night Michelle was conceived.

David had been thrilled to hear Margaret was pregnant. Margaret was confident she could manage her career, home, and the new arrival. David, however, did not approve of Margaret working. He eventually agreed to a reduction of her hours, after the baby arrived. Michelle was born without complications, David was there with flowers, chocolates, and a beautiful wicker crib. The nurses all commented what a lovely family they were, everything just as it should be. When Michelle was six months old, David arrived home from work early. Margaret had been alone all day, Michelle was teething, she needed constant attention. Over-tiredness and concern for the baby had left Margaret exhausted. Margaret was asleep on the sofa with Michelle beside her in the cot. David slammed the door, both Margaret and Michelle woke with a start. David began his daily inspection of the house. He removed the baby's clothing from the floor, where Margaret had left it. He inspected the house for dust, running his fingers along the top of shelves and behind the TV, tutting as he went. He then got the shopping receipt from the kitchen noticeboard, checked through all the purchases, products, and costs. He originally started doing this when Margaret had requested more housekeeping, the price of food was increasing, she had explained. His obsession about spending, his weekly checks, always brought a shiver of fear to Margaret. This week he said he was pleased she had saved over two pounds, using coupons and offers. He returned the receipt to the kitchen. Then he saw the trash bin was full. He was so angry, he ranted and shouted about hygiene, bacteria, and germs, how she was an unfit mother. Margaret made a gentle sarcastic reply, 'Maybe some help would be good'.

"Just look at you, you have become a lazy, scruffy slob. What the hell did I see in you?" He snarled down at her, Michelle began crying again, Margaret did not have the energy for another row. Every week, sometimes two or three times a week, there were arguments. She could never please him. David took Michelle and went out of the room. One hour later Margaret found him in the nursery, Michelle was asleep in his arms, he was staring in adoration. He loved Michelle, she had a calming influence on him, she was his special girl. After a few days, David said Margaret was not coping, with running the home and the baby. He insisted it would be better if Margaret gave up work to be at home. Margaret eventually agreed to put her career on hold.

David started to include Margaret in his daily inspections, her dress, her hair, her make-up. He said as her friends were not married and did not have children, it was inappropriate for Margaret to spend time with them. Although Margaret argued, about her freedom and rights to choose her own friends, he drilled his views home at every opportunity. He intercepted her calls, checked her text messages. Once he sent her best friend Sara away, telling her Margaret was not home and she did not really want to see Sara, she was too busy and quite frankly, felt they had nothing in common any more. Margaret learned of this when she contacted Sara later for a catch-up.

He was attentive and caring, the surprises continued. A trip to the theatre, David arranged for his mother to babysit. A romantic meal out, a day at the beach with Michelle and quiet evenings home with a glass of wine in the garden. Little gifts appeared, mostly for Michelle, Teddy bears, toys, and books. Occasionally, a new scarf or a bottle of perfume for Margaret. When Michelle was just four, they discussed schooling, David wanted the best for his daughter. Private schools cost money, so Margaret suggested she might return to work. David was livid, Margaret was needed at home, did she not remember how she let things slide when she was working. He could provide, didn't she think he took care of them? The argument lasted for two weeks, finally one evening David was in a foul mood, he did not want to eat what Margaret had made for supper, he threw it across the kitchen. Spaghetti bolognese, hit the white kitchen blind, tomato sauce ran down the window and wall. Margaret was frightened, he was possessed, he was now smashing cups and plates, he slammed her into the cupboard with such force she thought her arm was broken. He charged out of the room shouting, "Clean that mess up!!" Margaret cleaned the kitchen, her arm ached, she cried with the pain. The next day he agreed to take her to the hospital. They confirmed her arm was fractured, she needed a cast, it would need at least six weeks to heal.

David cried that night, he said he truly regretted what he had done, he had been stressed about changes at work, they were changing the distribution, it meant he would need to be away from home frequently. He said he was sorry and begged her forgiveness. Somewhere in her head Margaret was relieved he would be home less often. That night David needed her, she loved him, held him, then she conceived Daniel.

David was so happy, a proud Dad, he was already making plans for Daniel's future. Football, rugby, and tennis. He would of course join Michelle at private school. Daniel's Christening was a big event, all the family were invited along

with David's colleagues from work. Margaret was allowed extra money to buy supplies for the party, which would be held in their garden. When David's mother requested an extra piece of cake, for a distant aunt who could not attend, there was none.
This later was the basis of a full-blown argument, David complained that the entire day had been ruined because of her incompetence, her inability to order a cake large enough. Margaret tried to protest but soon realised it was pointless. David spent two nights in the spare room, speaking to her only when the children were there, with spiteful and derisory comments. Their lives settled into a pattern, Margaret mastered the 'specification list'and learned to anticipate mood changes.

David spent three days a week away from home and at weekends he was the perfect father, he took Daniel to football practice, cheering him on. Michelle kept busy with her friends and David provided a taxi service for her, to netball, swimming, or visits to her doting grandparents. The arguments were far less, due to the separation.

Margaret longed to go back to work, so one evening she raised the subject. This sparked another argument. Daniel and Michelle were both out. David had just got out of the shower and was getting ready; he was singing something by Elvis. Margaret mentioned returning to work. David's temper escalated immediately, he ranted and shouted abuse, his language became obscene, he pushed her on to the bed, he slapped her, taunted her. He was too heavy, too strong. He tore at her clothes, ripping her dress. She screamed. His fist split her lip. Her sobbing was so intense it was choking her, he tugged her hair, pulling so hard her head was on fire. All the time he was shouting, she was a slapper, a whore, she deserved this. With one last effort she tried to push him off, his right fist hit her with such force she literally saw stars. The room was spinning, then everything was black. Vaguely, she heard him laughing, as he entered her, the pain seared through her. She hated him.

Margaret made an appointment with her doctor two days later, her black eye, bruising and split lip were starting to heal. She was struggling with pain, whenever she passed water, it was like knives were ripping her apart. The doctor was curious where the bruising came from, Margaret lied and made up an elaborate tale about falling downstairs. An examination found bruising and skin damage around her vagina, the doctor said the damage was typical of rape victims, again questioning Margaret and offering confidential advice. Margaret maintained her story; she was given cream and antibiotics.

To the world David was the perfect husband, father, and provider. Margaret realised he had full control over his temper, he could switch it on and off like a tap. Prince Charming, the life and soul of the party. Publicly 'Mister Nice Guy'. Behind closed doors, in private, a tyrant, a bully, a controller. The children were unaware of David's dual personality, they only ever saw their kind, generous, loving Father.

One day whilst at the supermarket, Margaret was feeling fragile and low. David had gone on business to Sheffield and would not be home till Friday evening. Giving her four days respite. She touched her eye, sore from the collision with the fireplace. The eye had now turned black and there was a small gash just above the eyebrow. This 'punishment' was because she had not ironed his pale blue shirt and he needed it in Sheffield. The children were out, Michelle was at netball practice and Daniel was at his friend's house. When they saw her eye earlier this morning she had lied and said she stumbled against the fireplace, both children accepted this. Daniel with concern, Michelle with disdain. Michelle had seen so many of 'mother's accidents,' she thought Margaret clumsy and awkward.

As Margaret placed the shopping in the boot of the car, she decided to take a few moments and sit on the bench, her head hurt, her confidence was low. What had happened to her? Where was the Margaret she remembered, smiling, singing always happy? The thought suddenly popped into her head, 'I need a drink'. She went back into the store and bought a small, one serving, can of Vodka and tonic, for one pound forty-five. She sat on the bench and drank, it tasted good.

That was how it started.

The following week she bought three of the small tins, one she drank in the car park, the other two she carefully hid away in the back of the cleaning cupboard under the sink. This was her emergency 'medication' when she needed a boost, needed to feel stronger, needed to cope with his demands. The following week, when she returned to buy her secret supply, always on a separate receipt, the large bottle of vodka was on special offer. She could hardly drink from the bottle in the car park, so she bought the bottle for home and two tins for the car park. Back home the bottle was useful, Margaret had some control, something to fall back on. A little sip before or after his outbursts. She had read somewhere that vodka did not leave a smell on the breath, however, just to be sure, she always bought some extra strong mints. At first the straight vodka did not taste nice, however, it did work quickly and made her feel relaxed. That week David was angry, things had not been going well at work, angry because of the food Margaret cooked, angry that there was a coffee stain on the worktop and intensely angry that the man from the gas company, had charged fifty pounds to service the boiler.

Margaret washed the dishes after dinner, David came up behind, he had been making a cup of coffee, he yelled at her, she should have checked the price, why did she not get a quote from the local plumber. Did she think money grew on trees? Then, he accidentally, or was it deliberately? Poured boiling water into the bowl, scalding her hand. He smiled as she screamed. Michelle called from the other room, "What's going on in there, I can't hear myself think?" David replied, "It's OK darling, Mum just spilled some hot water on her hand." The back of Margaret's hand was bright red from her thumb to her third finger. She winced in pain, she fought the urge to scream or cry. She tried desperately to hold her hand under the running cold water to ease the pain. Later that evening, when everyone was asleep, Margaret slipped downstairs and had a large glass of Vodka. How could she have been so stupid, she should have known it would make David angry, she should have spoken to him first before paying the gas man.

Some weeks later, David came home early from a trip. Margaret was alone in the house. David realised something was wrong, Margaret was slurring her speech and walking unsteadily. His rage poured out, "Where did she get the alcohol? Who had she been out with? Where did she get money for drink from? Who paid? Did she steal from the housekeeping?" He shouted, he searched the house looking for evidence, he threw everything out of the drawers on the floor. He found an empty bottle, concealed inside a used soap powder box, in the recycling bin. He lost control, "So you are a Drunken Slut now." He pulled her from the chair, dragged her up the staircase, into the bathroom He then filled the bath with water. Margaret sat bemused, she did not understand why he was so upset or why they were in the bathroom. He easily picked her up, fully clothed he unceremoniously dropped her in the bath. the water was ice cold. "This will soon sober you up" he sneered. He sat on the toilet seat and watched as Margaret shivered and cried, long hard sobs. Every attempt to get out, to stand, he pushed her head under the water. Fighting for breath Margaret gasped, "I'm sorry, I only had one glass, please." She yelped like a wounded animal. "Liar, liar, liar. You are a liar, a drunken liar." He got a bottle of bleach from the shelf and attempted to pour it in the water, Margaret scrambled to get out. The bleach did not pour easily, David threw the bottle in the water and stormed out, crashing the door closed behind him. Margaret slowly climbed out of the bath and locked the door. She sat and waited, tears still flowing. She could not hear him. Slowly she started to take the cold wet clothes off and wrap herself in the towel. It was three thirty, the children were due home in a few minutes, she decided to wait until then to come out of the bathroom, then it would be safe.

Things returned to normal for a few days, though at every opportunity, David added sly whispers of, "got any more stashes?" "How long can you survive without a drink?" "Missing the Vodka, slut?" Margaret tried to ignore him, he might calm down, he might forgive her. She must show him she is really trying to do everything right. Tuesday evening, she has made lasagne, a family favourite with side salad and garlic bread. The children had their supper early, Michelle had homework and Daniel wanted to play on his new computer game. David arrived at seven, he did not look happy. Margaret had tried, she has tied her hair back and wore a black top, which she had bought years ago, it always felt nice, figure flattering, David had confirmed this once in a romantic moment. David looked at the table set for two, Margaret was putting the food out. He said he did not want any food, that she looked like a tart, she could not cook, he had already eaten. With a final cut he said, "Why would I want to eat with a slut?" He went to bed.

The following week Margaret purchased her usual bottle of Vodka, she would have to be more careful, the three tins of vodka and tonic went down well. Margaret smiled as she watched the other shoppers rushing around, filling their trolleys with groceries. Was this what she had signed up for? Housework, childcare, cooking and cleaning? What happened to her dreams? She had wanted to travel to visit foreign lands, the furthest she had been was their honeymoon to Sri Lanka. That had been beautiful, the best. They had been so much in love then. When did it change? Had it been so gradual she had not noticed. He had always been persuasive, he chose the honeymoon destination, the colour of the bridesmaid dresses, he had written most of her wedding vows. All these things were done with loving concern, he always wanted the best for her.
This large bottle of Vodka was to be stored in the cupboard under the stairs, there were boxes of old picture frames and a stack of tiles from the kitchen make-over, she hid the bottle behind them.

The weeks turned into months, Margaret learned to lie, to be devious, to hide what had now become a desperate need for a drink. So much so, that she had pawned her grandmother's jewellery to pay for alcohol.

Often when David came home, he recognised Margaret had been drinking, sometimes he ignored her, sometimes he hit her, sometimes he just humiliated her. When Margaret slurred her words, her drunken behaviour was different, more defiant, confident almost fearless. He had now added searches of the house, to his daily routine. David like a man obsessed, determined to discover where the hidden supplies were.

Margaret watched carefully; did she finish the last bottle? She could not remember. Did she have any more hidden away? Where did she put the large bottle last week, she was sure she had not drunk that, not all of it. She smiled as she remembered how clever she had been, taking the panel off the side of the bath and hiding it under there. David was slamming around the house, under the stairs, moving boxes. He came into the kitchen, carrying an empty bottle and one bottle half full. He was livid. "What in hell's name are you playing at, you think you are hiding it from me, do you, do you?" He was shaking her violently at this point and Margaret could feel the bile rising in her throat. He let go, Margaret began to slide off the seat and sat in the middle of the kitchen floor. He charged out of the room and upstairs. Margaret could hear him in their bedroom, in the bathroom. He even climbed into the loft space, Margaret smiled, as if she would hide it there, she would never be able to get a drink. Then he is in Daniel's room, Daniel, she would never hide anything in there, what if Daniel had found it? What if he knew his mother was drinking? Did he know she had been drinking? When she went to the book day at school, she remembered, she had a small drink before leaving.

She could not recall much about the day. The nosey busy body, whose daughter was in Daniel's class, had asked, "Are you alright dear, you look a bit unsteady, is there anything I can do". Margaret had dismissed her with a glare and stumbled into a seat on the second row. Did Daniel see? Suddenly Margaret felt sad, what had she done, she should not be drinking, especially not when planning a visit to the school, no wonder David was so mad. Daniel was probably angry too. Then David appeared at the door with four more bottles, two almost empty, one full, one a quarter full. Margaret sighed, he had got all her stash, who did he think he was, it was her life, her body, her choice. David tipped all the alcohol into the sink, "Bastard," Margaret whispered. David turned on her. "What? What? You stupid cow. You are an alcoholic; don't you see that? You have ruined everything, the kids hate you, I hate you, you have no friends. You are just a drunken waste of space." David threw the glass he was holding against the wall; he then ran his hand along the shelf bringing the cups and plates crashing to the floor. He kicked the trash bin over and tossed a chair across the room. She was scared but a little voice in her head told her to fight back. Margaret slowly stood up; she was still a bit wobbly. "Oh really, it's me is it? All my fault you selfish controlling pig." Before the last word had left her lips, Margaret felt the crushing blow of David's fist against her chin, her head flicked backwards as though it were on a spring. Maybe the alcohol gave her more strength, she stood her ground. A slap across the face sent her reeling across the room, still she was on her feet. She could hear the obscenities pouring from his mouth. He picked up the carving knife and wielded it in the air, glaring at her. Who was this man? The thought flashed through Margaret's mind. Her survival instinct kicked in, she tugged at the door handle, pulled the door open, David started towards her. Once out on the driveway, Margaret desperately cried out, "Help, help me please, somebody help me." Margaret did not see what happened next, a pain shot through her face, she fell to the floor. Drifting out of reality, she had heard him. David was crying, he was explaining to the someone through his tears. Something warm was covering her face. Then it all went black.

Later she learned, two neighbours had intervened, pulled David away. David had convinced the neighbours Margaret had been on a drunken rampage. smashed the house up. Then she had attacked him, as he tried to take a knife away from her. He was distraught, he did not know why she was being like this, he did not even know she had a drink problem. As he tried to take the knife from her, he could not believe, she slashed it against her own face, he said incredulously, she actually wanted to harm herself. He then cried out harder. He wanted to help her, she had been strange for weeks, even the children had noticed her odd behaviour. She had systematically pushed her family and friends away. One neighbour consoled David, the other gave directions to the ambulance. This time Margaret accepted help, a refuge for women, though she still refused to press charges.

Margaret woke up, not knowing where she was? Why she was so cold? What day it was? She lifted her head. She was lying on cold damp tarmac, in the middle of a road. Trying to stand, she has no idea, how she got there in the middle of a road. She struggled to her feet. Her clothes were dirty and wet, her hair hung limp around her face, it had been raining.

Margaret felt frightened and lost. What had she become? What did her future hold?

**First Visit**

I have just had a week on annual leave, with Paul my best friend and current partner, a glorious week in Rhodes, a fantastic Greek island. We lay on the beach, ate too much, drank too much wine, and generally indulged in each other. I never thought I could feel like this again. Carla Saxon, I say to myself, behave! You are over forty and behaving like a sixteen-year-old. It was extremely hard to get out of bed; Paul had spent the night but today we both have work to go to.

I wear a white blouse, this shows off my new tan, I tie

my hair up in a tight knot and add just a little lipstick. Ready for the office, I am a little disappointed to find there is only Bill, my manager in when I arrive. "Good morning", he laughs "Wow, do you have any white bits?" I playfully push him away, "Your jokes are even older than you," I grin.

I spend the morning catching up on my caseload, checking everyone is safe and well. I have forty-two clients allocated to me at the moment, it is too many, but I would rather be busy, plus I quite enjoy the challenge. Just before lunch the team start to filter back into the office. Alan smiles, "Welcome back partner, I have a few things I'd like to go through with you, when you're ready." I can tell it is nothing urgent, Alan panics if there is a real problem. Sandra and Shirley come in with fish and chips, the food smells delicious, I should have asked them to bring me some.

Lacey comes crashing in with her usual flamboyancy, today's attire is a red and gold patterned dress, which falls in layers of soft cheesecloth to just below the knee. On her head is a matching turban, which for some peculiar reason, does not look the least bit out of place. She is holding a half-eaten Cornish pasty. Mike and Alan walk straight through to the kitchen.

It is rare for everyone to be in at the same time, there are thirty members of the carer team and four dedicated social workers. The latter have their own office but frequently pop in to find out client information or to work on the computers. With only twelve computers it is a struggle sometimes to get a seat. We are a happy bunch, in general. In this type of work, you have to know who is who, who will have your back if there is a problem, who will only work within the rules, who will go the extra mile. Unfortunately, there are some who prefer to do as little as possible, however, when there is a serious problem, everyone pulls their weight.

The chatter dies down as people enjoy their lunch, most people are working as they eat, not a good practice but a common one. At around two o'clock my phone rings, it's Gordon, a social worker linked to the drugs and alcohol team. He asks me if I can do him a favour. Gordon is old school social worker and has not really adapted to technology. A great people person though, with lots of empathy. Aged fifty-eight, after twenty-five years in the service, he is now planning his retirement.

"I just had the district nurse on the phone; concerned about a woman on the Heald Estate. Apparently, this lady is not eating properly, they are worried about her health, she is a drinker, no family, lives alone in the flats, you know the high-rise block?" Gordon is vague about the client. "I haven't time today I am in court this afternoon. Could you just pop round, take her a sandwich and some crisps, just so we know she has something to eat. I will visit her first thing in the morning to prepare a care package, I would really appreciate this." Gordon sounds a little stressed, I am still in holiday mode, so I agree to go. Gordon gives me the address and sends me the link for her file. I will have a quick read before I go out. Her file is slim, her case was reported to the district nurse by a neighbour, who was concerned for the client's welfare. Unknown people had been seen going to the flat at odd hours, there was alcohol involved, in large quantities. The neighbour asked for medical help because they were concerned, the lady was looking 'unwell'. The district nurses had been unable to get a response at the flat. The neighbours said they had seen the client make trips to the shops on a daily basis. After three unsuccessful visits the district nurses made the referral.

So, here she was, my new client her name was Margaret Unwin, aged fifty-five, no medical records available. I assume this will just be a call to provide food, and leave. Most drinkers do not want social services or any other agency involved.

I should know never to assume anything in this job.

I dislike these flats, built in the sixties the tower blocks hold no attraction for me, some say that they have fantastic views, the higher they live. I never really liked the idea of opening my front door into a corridor, where all doors looked the same. This block had been through a series of changes and modernisation. Now the flats have supposedly working lifts, new fire, health and safety provisions and a facelift, which although completed only two years ago, is already covered with graffiti, the work of some talented artists. Subject matter for the diagrams, the anatomy of mankind. The lifts do not look new. I check my notes, the lady lives on the second floor. I press the button. As I wait for the lift an elderly woman arrives, she is dressed in a grey overcoat, probably a size too big, she has a purple woolly hat pulled down over her ears. We wait. As we get into the lift there is a strong stench of urine, the interior has also been visited by the felt tip pen, 'I Was Here,' artist. I ask the woman which floor, she replies, "second." She smiles at me, I notice her lips are dry and cracked, there is a dark tide line around her neck, I suspect the smell of urine is not all from the lift compartment. We leave the lift, the woman walks unsteadily ahead down the long dim corridor, weighed down on each side by heavy carrier bags. I check the door numbers; she stops outside the flat I am looking for.

"Hello, are you Margaret?" I ask, thinking that this

woman seems much older than fifty-five, by at least ten years. She turns to me, and says "Yes, that's me. Who are you? And what do you want?"

"Hi, my name is Carla, I work for social services. We received a call from the district nurses, they are concerned about you. Could we have a chat please?" Margaret opens the door and steps inside, she goes to close the door then stops,

"What is it you want?" she asks accusingly.

"Nothing, nothing at all. I have brought you a sandwich and some crisps, just thought we could have a chat?" I wait as Margaret calculates 'sandwich or slam the door', the sandwich wins, she goes in, I follow.

The flat has a terrible stench, it takes my breath away as I follow her down the hallway. To the right is a door, I know will lead to the kitchen, to my left the bathroom. A bedroom and living room are at the rear of the property, overlooking a park area. Margaret takes her off coat and hat, tosses them over a pile of other clothes on an armchair. She sits down on another chair, located a couple of feet away from a wall mounted electric fire. She invites me to sit down. The room is untidy, with mismatched pieces of furniture. Margaret is a smoker; the windows bear a nicotine coating.

I watch Margaret as she unpacks her carrier bags. She was once a very good-looking woman. I can see her high cheek bones, her shapely lips, and her ice blue eyes. Her hair is greying now, there are traces of black and brown hues. It looks as though a cut and wash are long overdue. Her clothing is dirty, stains of previous spillages and accidents. Margaret looks underweight, without the large overcoat she is a very petite lady. She removes six large bottles of cider from the carrier bags and places them on the floor at the side of her chair. I look around, where can I sit? As the other armchair is full of clothing, the settee is the only option. On one side the cushion is collapsed in, I fear if I sit on it, I will sink to the floor. The centre cushion is covered in towels, they are wet. I realise they are wet with urine. The third cushion is stacked high with magazines and old newspapers. I walk towards the kitchen, "I will get you a plate for your sandwich." I offer. Margaret asks, "Could you get me a glass too."

I open the door to be greeted by a swarm of flies, there are hundreds of them. On the table is an assortment of rotted food, also covered in flies. The sink is stacked with pots and pans. The window over the sink is covered in flies, the window sill is a fly graveyard. The cooker is in pieces, there are no controls, I investigate further and realise it is not connected to the mains. She has no method of cooking. The cooker is so full of grease the hotplates are hidden. I quickly rinse a glass under the tap, there are no clean plates. I use the napkin supplied by the shop as a plate. I keep the kitchen door closed; we are going to need some expert help with cleaning. As I return to the living room, I reach out for the handle, then stop myself, it is coated in dried on faeces. I feel my last meal rising in my throat.

Margaret accepts the glass and quickly fills it with cider, it is not like any cider I have seen before, this is clear, almost like water. Margaret starts to make a roll up cigarette, she does this with precision, something she has probably done a million times. I decide I should look at the rest of the flat.

"Is it OK for me to use your bathroom please? I have been out all morning and well - needs must." I try to sound casual.

"Toilet's broke, sorry." She replies. I decide not to be distracted and say "Oh, maybe I can fix it." with that I disappear down the hall to the bathroom. As I open the door the stench is sickening, like walking into an open sewer. The toilet is blocked but that has not prevented usage. I look in the bath, there is a large cardboard box with a black plastic bin bag inside, loosely folded over. I carefully open the top of the bag, the box is full of urine and faeces, I gag and cover it over. This is a makeshift toilet, I am impressed with her ingenuity, sickened by the vulgarity of it. There are smears all over the wall and door. During her bouts of drinking she has struggled to stand, let alone support herself over the box, cleaning herself must have been haphazard, this woman is in a mess. I return to the living room. I notice the large blue bottles circling around the top light and gathering at the window. I am sure I have seen this in a horror film.

"Margaret, how long has the toilet been broken?" I ask. She stares into space, calculating, "About three months, I guess. I reported it twice, but no one came." She poured another glass of cider. "Want a drop?" she offers, I shake my head. "Would you like me to get it fixed?" I know these properties are owned by the local authority. Margaret nods her head. "You might have better luck than me." She shrugs.

"So how long have you lived here Margaret?" I am intrigued how she can live like this.

"About seven years I reckon, don't come from this part of town, moved here, yeah must have been seven maybe eight years ago". She takes another swig of her cider.

"So, where do you originate from? This is not an official interview, a social worker will come and take your details tomorrow, so you do not have to tell me. I'm just interested." I am speaking truthfully, there is something about this women I like, I think it may be her openness, or her relaxed manner or maybe I am just a sucker for a hard luck story. Margaret smiles, "I have nothing to hide, I lived over in Higher Coombe, do you know it? "I nod, I know it is one of the most expensive areas of town, lots of people from the TV, actors and presenters live there, some footballers too.

"Yes, I expect you are thinking, this woman is spinning me a tale, she is nothing but a drunk. I tell you I had one of those big houses once. "Margaret stares into her glass and I realise she likes to talk. She begins to tell me her story," I was happy once," she gazes into space and continues," Margaret and David Unwin, were married in a church. Both families attended…

"Did you ever get in touch with your children again?" I ask. "Yes, when I was in the hostel, it was in the centre of Liverpool you know, never realised how nice the people in that part of the world are, very friendly and caring. I did not stop drinking but I slowed down, did not have the cash, had nothing but the clothes I was wearing when I arrived. I made friends with a woman in there, she rang my daughter Michelle for me. Michelle said she did not want to see me ever again but promised to try and get some of my things out of the house, she refused to speak to me. She never rang back, changed her number. I was so hurt, I took my weekly allowance and spent it all on a two-day drinking binge.

Then a few weeks later I woke up in the middle of the road. My drinking became a real problem, I was so desperate I started to steal money from the other girls in the hostel, to buy drink. After several warnings they told me I had to leave. I was homeless for a while." "The scar on your cheek?" I watch as Margaret runs her fingers over the three- inch scar, which just misses her eyes. "Yes, that was my parting gift from David." Margaret is back there, somewhere in her past, tears fill her eyes. Two hours later, I leave. Margaret's story has touched me, I feel for her, for every woman who finds herself trapped in an abusive relationship. I decide I would like to work with her. During my visit Margaret has finished a bottle and a half of cider. Not being much of a drinker myself I realise that I would be very drunk after one or two glasses where as she appears sober.

On the drive back to the office I consider Margaret's story, this could happen to any woman. Alcohol was her way of escaping, some women turn to anti-depressants, some just stay until their partners kill them or mentally break them. When I was young, alcohol was a sort of 'growing -up', 'coming of age 'ritual, the aim to get drunk. I can remember buying a bottle of cider from the off licence, with two friends. We had each contributed to the cost, one friend provided ten Embassy filter cigarettes (stolen from her parents). We took our contraband to the local park, found a quiet, secluded spot, and shared the cider, whist puffing away on the cigarettes. We were twelve years old.

I never got really drunk until I reached the age of fifteen. By that age I would go in the local public bars, lots of friends my age did, if they were brave enough. Not only did we manage to get served, often we were allowed to stay after hours. The night I got drunk, I was trying 'Babycham', meant to be a sort of 'mock' champagne. I do not know how many I had, I remember listening to 'ABC' by The Jackson Five, followed by George Harrison singing 'My Sweet Lord'. Then the room seemed fuzzy, I heard someone say, "She needs to go outside."

The next thing I knew, I was projectile vomiting said Babycham and contents of my last meal across the table, floor, and the person opposite. Someone, half carried, half pushed me outside. I vaguely remember the landlord shouting that I was barred and should never come back, something about ruining a new carpet. I never did go back in that bar, well not for twenty-five years.

During my life I have enjoyed celebrating with a drink, however, I realised very quickly that too much alcohol, removes all my inhibitions. This in itself can have consequences.

I once met a guy at a nightclub, not really my type, a little older, I was nineteen. He bought me drinks the entire evening. I danced with friends, returning to his company for a drink. At the end of the evening I sneaked off without even saying goodbye to him. In those days' men were like jobs, there were lots to choose from. I was young and enjoying life. Monday morning, I had an interview for a position in a local factory. I arrived at reception and asked for Mr Quinn, who was the manager. It could only happen to me, there in front of me wearing a pristine white overall, is the man from the nightclub. He looked at me, then said accusingly, "It's you!" I mumbled some excuse, sorry had to leave, my friend was not well, I did not have time to come back. He smiled. "I suppose this means I will not get the job?" I fluttered my eyes at him, hoping for a little sympathy. Thankfully, he was very understanding, I worked for the company for just over a year.

Back at the office I speak to Bill, explain a rough outline of the situation, asking if I might be Margaret's allocated Support Worker, he agrees. I then ring Gordon.
"Hi Gordon, yes I visited her, and 'Houston I think we might

have a problem' there is a lot of work to be done with this lady!" I love a challenge. I agree to meet Gordon at the flat the next day.

Paul and I decide not to see each other this evening, we both needed time alone after our holiday, time to reassess where we are going, if anywhere. We enjoy each other's company; the sex is brilliant too. However, we have both been on our own for so long, we enjoy our independence. Do we need to be any more committed than that? I have my shower and relax on the sofa; the holiday washing still sits in the bag. I have cold chicken from the supermarket and a pre-packed salad. Mr. Tom lies curled up on my lap. I switch on the news, the next thing I know it is the end of a programme about the Amazon rainforest, shame, I would have enjoyed it. I flick the TV off.

Now I am refreshed after my power nap of over an hour. I start to think of possible agencies able to help Margaret. My laptop is great for research. The first obvious two are the AA, Alcoholics Anonymous, or the Drugs and Alcohol Services, provided by the local authority in conjunction with the National Health Service. There is also the Salvation Army who are noted for their work in the town, involved with the homeless, drug addicts and alcohol abusers. I know of an excellent cleaning company locally, they have cleaned a few houses at my request, specialists in deep cleaning, they also offer fumigation and pest control.

Margaret mentioned her family, she had not seen them since the day the ambulance took her away. She had understood from the brief conversation between her new friend and Michelle, that the children did not want to see her, they blamed her for everything. That was a long time ago, people forget, they mature; maybe there will be a chance of reconciliation with the children?

The question is will Margaret co-operate with us? Many alcoholics either deny they have a problem or convince themselves that this is the life they want. It is often extremely difficult for them to acknowledge they require help, then to comply with the help.

When medical intervention is required there are organisations like RADAR, who work within the Greater Manchester area, to provide rapid access for patients from acute wards, in general hospitals across the area. They offer detoxification programmes, quick acting programmes of five to seven days, they offer psychological therapies and interventions, working with relapse and prevention. The idea being to reduce the pressure on the National Health Service. Alcohol misuse is the biggest risk factor for death, ill health, and disability among fifteen to forty-nine year old, in the UK and the fifth biggest risk factor across all ages. I read this on the website for RADAR. The problem is escalating, alcohol, unlike heroin or cocaine, is openly available on every high street and can be purchased legally, providing you are eighteen. I wonder if Margaret understands the risks. If she gives a damn? When she left David, she lost everything, he took away her life, her future, her hope. She has no self-esteem, confidence, or willpower. It is like everything that made her human was systematically sucked out of her and she replaced it with alcohol, a depressant, a one-way ticket. Alcohol does not care how clever or knowledgeable you are, how wealthy or poor, how young, or old it takes whoever is willing.

Mr. Tom stretches, its already past midnight, I glance at my phone. A message from Paul "Sleep well my love, see you tomorrow. Miss you." The message was sent at nine o'clock. I decide to wait till morning to reply.

**Second Visit**

Gordon is outside the flats when I arrive, he looks the part of a traditional 'social worker', wearing jeans, tee shirt and leather strappy sandals, thankfully he is not wearing socks. Already grey; his hair sits on his shoulders and he has a bushy grey beard. He has thick rimmed glasses and smokes a pipe, but not when on duty. We go to the flat together. Margaret's door is open, we knock and hear Margaret call 'come in'. Once in the living room Gordon does the usual "Hello I am Gordon your allocated Social Worker, this is Carla whom you met yesterday".

With introductions done, Gordon sits down on the centre of the sofa. I inwardly cringe, the towels there are soaked by weeks, maybe months of urine. I wonder should I say something, he is in full stream now chatting away with Margaret. I wonder how long before the dampness will start to penetrate his jeans. I crouch down on the floor. "Why don't you sit at this end, where the magazines are, Margaret can see you better then?" I suggest. Gordon smiles and tells me he is fine where he is, and wriggles further into the cushion to prove his point. You just cannot help some people. "But I think the cushion might be a little damp?" He waves his hand, "I am fine." Gordon asks Margaret a lot of questions, directly to the point.
"How many bottles of cider do you drink a day?" He is making notes. "Three, sometimes more. Depends how many I buy." Margaret grins.

I notice four empty bottles at the side of her chair which were not there yesterday. On the table is a full bottle and Margaret has a glass at the side of her, which she sips periodically. "Did you eat breakfast this morning?" I decide alcohol on an empty stomach is not good. Margaret looks at me as though I said something in Russian. "No, did you?" she answers. "Well yes actually I did". Obviously, breakfast to Margaret is a rarity. Gordon continues, "Do you have many visitors here Margaret?" "No, Jim from across the way calls in on Fridays to see if I want anything from the market, he usually has a quick drink with me before he goes. Oh and of course she comes now and then. She does not stay long - sometimes hides behind that chair. She is very shy, won't come out if there are people about." Margaret looks thoughtful.

We ask more about the female visitor, Margaret is vague, she says it is a young girl, about ten or twelve maybe, who lives nearby, she comes to talk to Margaret because she is lonely. She is small and always wears her hair tied in pigtails, wears some really pretty dresses. She talks about her friends, the sunshine, her father. Both Gordon and I say we would love to meet her, when will she next call. Margaret explains she is not sure, sometimes she comes late at night, sometimes early morning.

Gordon and I are considering the possibility this young 'visitor' is an hallucination. Alcoholic hallucinations can occur twenty-four hours after the last intake of alcohol, they can continue for up to twenty-four hours in the form of visual, auditory, and tactile hallucinations. In advance stages these hallucinations can be perceived as real, then they may become threatening or frightening and can increase anxiety. Patients at this stage can pull or touch imaginary objects. This is not necessarily followed by the DTs, (Delirium Tremens), commonly known as the shakes. It is possible that, when not able to meet her

alcohol intake, Margaret's body goes into withdrawal, it responds with hallucinations of a young girl, which explains the odd times and infrequency. Gordon asks Margaret "Have you ever tried to get help with your drinking?" Margaret finishes the cider in her glass. "Yes, a few times. I got a bit of help from the Salvation Army; they took me to Church and gave me food and clothes. Really nice people. Oh, and I tried the AA meeting a few years ago, we came out of the meeting and went for a drink, so that didn't work either." Gordon then asks "Margaret, do you want to stop drinking?" She looks sad and stares at the floor, then she looks at me. There is not that big an age difference, Margaret looks a lot older, her skin has a yellow tinge, she is underweight, her eyes are dull, no sparkle. Her hair is lank and greasy, and she is dressed in clothes many would tear up as rags. She looks back at Gordon and says "Yes, of course I do. It's hard!!" "I know it's hard Margaret, but we want to help you, we can support you every day to get you through this, we can get you help, medication, counselling. Whatever it takes if you are willing to co-operate. "I look to Gordon for confirmation, he nods.
Margaret smiles, "Let's give it a go then."

**Third Visit**

The office helpline received a call today from a member of the public, a lady, asking for support with her husband. It is unusual to get direct referrals, there is an established procedure. However, it is not unheard of, we accept the referral. Later telephone calls are made to clear the 'protocol' with other departments. I am asked to visit the lady and look at the needs, assess what, if any, support package is needed. Apparently her husband is ill.

I arrive at the house which is situated in a respectable

area of the town, it is a semi-detached, smartly presented property. The lady who answers the door is in her sixties, a smart and attractive women, with short grey hair. I introduce myself. Her name is Maureen Hall, she looks at me and asks, "So, where are you from? "I explain I have come from social services to discuss a possible care package. The lady looks stressed, on the verge of tears. "I suppose you better come in." she says resolutely.

I follow Maureen through the lounge into the kitchen, she grabs the kettle, "Tea? Or would you prefer coffee?" I choose tea. As we wait for the kettle, I can feel the tension, something is not right. "Are you alright Mrs Hall?" I ask. She immediately looks at me, then bursts into tears, she is distraught, her shoulders shake with the sheer weight of her sobs. I quickly stand and place my arm around her shoulder, "I am sorry, come and sit down, let me see if I can help." I finish making the tea, by which time her crying had subsided a little and she is wiping her eyes. "Sorry, I am not usually this emotional" she sniffs. "It's just that so many people have been, I am an independent person and now I feel lost, I don't think I can cope with much more." I explain to Maureen that I am here to agree a support package for her and her husband. "It is not me that needs support, its George my husband, he will not get out of bed! I am exhausted getting him food, helping him to go to the toilet, washing him. No one seems to know what to do". Maureen is clearly very distressed.

"We can help with all those things, we really need George to be involved in the discussion, can we go and talk to him?" I need to know more about the nature of George's illness. We finish our tea; Maureen tells me she has been managing on her own for two weeks. They have a family, two sons and a daughter, both sons now live in New Zealand and her daughter lives in London. The daughter is trying to get time off work to come and help.

Upstairs George is lying in bed, he says hello but does not move, I explain why I am here, how I would really like to talk to him about his needs. I ask, "George, do you think you could sit up while we talk?" He gives a half smile, I can see he is a large man, probably around the same age as Maureen. "I can try." he offers. I go around to the side of the bed and ask Maureen if she can help. Before we can move him, he cries out in pain, it is clear any movement gives him excruciating pain.

"Alright George, we are not going to try and move you any more. How long have you been like this?" I ask. "Two weeks, since he fell out of bed." Maureen replies, she looks tired, worn out, literally at her wits end. "Two weeks ago? Has he seen a doctor?" I ask. Maureen gives a half smile "Oh yes, the day it happened, then again the week after. Gave him these pain killers," she points to two plastic bottles of tablets. "Then the nurse came and checked him. Then one of your lot came and talked to him. I feel as though I cannot carry on like this, I need help with him now." George cries out in pain again as he struggles to turn, "Don't get upset Mo, I will be OK." George says forcing a smile.

I take Maureen out of the bedroom, "Maureen I am going to ring for an ambulance, I think George needs to be checked." I start to dial as I speak. Maureen is concerned that I am overreacting, I assure her it is better to be safe than sorry, "I am not medically trained but I know that no one should be in this much pain." I say, trying to reassure her without causing panic. "I think the least they can do is x-ray George to ensure nothing's broken." I request an ambulance.

Twenty minutes later George is on a stretcher and headed for the hospital. Maureen is to follow in the car. "Please give me a call and let me know how George is. When he returns home, I will be pleased to arrange another visit to organise some support." I suggest. However, Maureen is juggling a thousand thoughts; I can see her stress, I am sure she has not heard.

Although I feel justified in ringing the ambulance, part of me is concerned that other professionals have judged him to be alright, not requiring further investigation. He was never given an x-ray after falling out of bed, which I find odd. I wonder if George is faking it, then dismiss the idea as ludicrous. I set off for my next visit, to Margaret.

When I arrive at Margaret's its almost lunchtime, she answers the door by calling "Come in". I wonder if she leaves her door on the latch all the time. Not a safe thing to do in this area. Margaret is smiling and cheerful, a little too cheerful and I wonder how much she has drunk. My plan is to take her to meet the team at the drug and alcohol service, to at least introduce her to the idea of getting professional help. I am not sure if they will want to see her if she is inebriated. I have asked Shirley, a member of our team, to meet me here, I would like her to meet Margaret. Shirley is the same age as Margaret, divorced and living alone. She is one hundred percent reliable; I know she cares deeply for all her clients; she always walks the extra mile for them. I am extremely pleased she will be working with Margaret.

"Hello Margaret, how are you today?" I smile, the smell in the flat is making me nauseous, it's mind over matter I tell myself. Margaret smiles, "I am fine. My little friend did not come last night, I hope her mother does not stop her from coming. "What are you here for? Do you have any tobacco?" I say I am sorry; I do not smoke. I notice there is just one empty bottle of cider by the chair. I remind Margaret why I am here "Do you remember I came yesterday with Gordon?" Margaret grins "Ah yes, that nice young man, where is he now?"

"Gordon asked me to visit today, with another member of our Team, Shirley. She should be here in about ten minutes. You remember we spoke about getting some help for you? I thought we might visit the alcohol services in town this afternoon. What do you think?" Margaret is busily cleaning grime from under her fingernails with a matchstick, I dare not even think about what the grime might be. Eventually she responds, "What can they do then?"

Shirley, my colleague, calls out "Hello." From the hallway, Margaret replies "Come in love, we are receiving visits in the throne room today". Shirley comes in, we make the introductions, Margaret is pleased when Shirley admits she smokes, although not allowed when she is on duty, she willingly offers Margaret a cigarette. Margaret insists one cigarette will be alright, she promises not to tell on Shirley. But she is professional, and declines.

I can see Shirley is struggling with the smell; she indicates to me that she wishes to go outside. "Sorry, Margaret we just have to make a call outside, be back in a minute." I make the excuse. Shirley is looking very pale, we walk to the lift, "I just need some fresh air, how do you bear it?" we go in the lift and outside. Shirley then vomits into the nearby drain. I am not good with vomit; I look away whilst fishing in my bag for a tissue. Shirley wipes her mouth, "Well, that's today's lunch gone". She still looks pale but agrees to come back in. I warn her not to go into the kitchen or bathroom.

"Hi Margaret, we are back. Sorry about that. You asked me about the alcohol services and what they do. They offer a confidential service for people who are affected by alcohol, they can give medical advice and treatments, they basically have programmes to help people stop drinking. There are lots of people who work there who have themselves been helped; they want to help others. They know and understand what the problems are. They operate a walk-in centre, where you can safely just pop in for a coffee and a chat, so you know you are not alone. What do you think Margaret?" I try to sound casual; I really need her to 'want' to come along.

Margaret considers my comments, then says, "Are they like the AA, where you all sit and talk. I didn't get along with them, went about five years ago, waste of time."

"I know that a lot of help organisations do use 'talking" as a therapy but it's not the only help available, I thought we could visit and take a look around. I rang them and we can go at two o'clock if you want to? Shirley and I will come with you, and there is no pressure. It is just a visit to see what you think. What do you say?" Margaret squashes her cigarette in the ashtray and says, "OK but they will have to take me as I am, what you see is what you get." With that Margaret laughs, "Don't suppose you can let me have another cigarette before we go?"

The three of us set off for town, Shirley and I are glad to leave the smell behind, though it feels like it has penetrated our clothes. The drug and alcohol services are based in an old Victorian building, I understand at one time it was an insurance company. The entrance is unassuming, there is a glass box on the wall containing details of opening hours, group meetings, talks and film shows. It could almost be the entrance to a youth club. Inside there is a small desk with a rather overweight gentleman sitting reading the paper. I explain who we are. He picks up the phone, "I'll just let them know you are here, I think Rob is doing the guided tours today, he gives a short laugh.

Rob, I estimate is in his early fifties, he gives a warm smile and invites us to follow him. Margaret does not appear phased by the place; she is taking everything in her stride. We are given coffee and Rob explains what is happening today at the centre. He directs his conversation at Margaret, she is giving him her full attention. Rob tells Margaret that after his wife divorced him, he started drinking, he was not sure at what point it became a problem. He had almost died, one-night walking home from the pub he was so drunk he stumbled and fell into the canal, he could not swim. Not the best place to drown he grinned. Fortunately, a young couple were also walking along the canal path, between them they managed to pull him out and call for an ambulance. "I remember I could not breathe, I thought this is it, I'm a goner. My chest was shutting down, I could not see, the water was freezing, I moved around splashing, trying to find something to hold on to. My instinct told me not to breathe under the water, I knew I was running out of air, I think I passed out. I owe my life to those two young people." For a moment Rob is back there in the canal, his face serious, thankful.

Margaret listens without comment. "So, I assume because you are here, you would like to take control of your drinking, am I right? Margaret looks at Rob and nods.
"Well, you are over the first hurdle, you know you have a

problem and secondly you want to do something about it. Do you know how much you drink in a week?" Rob leans back in the chair.

"I think, I think, sometimes I drink more than other days" Margaret is trying to be honest; I suspect she does not really know. "On average?" Rob prompts.

"I suppose I drink about six bottles." She whispers. "Right, that is six bottles a week?" Rob queries. "what is your preferred tipple?" Rob asks. "My preferred tipple is Champagne but I'm on a tight budget so it's Blue Lightening cider." She grins adding, "A day. Six a day. Wednesdays and Thursdays, I do not have any money, so sometimes I miss those days." Rob did not look surprised or judgemental, he continues his explanation of the service.

"We do not want you to stop drinking at this point, that will be too dangerous. Because your body is used to this amount of alcohol, to suddenly stop means you are likely to experience withdrawal symptoms. On the days you have no alcohol you may have experienced minor withdrawal symptoms, you may even experience a seizure, if you have not had a drink for say six hours. If you go for longer without a drink, say twelve to twenty-four hours, you could experience hallucinations. This can be frightening. After one or two days you may feel quite poorly, headaches, tremors and tummy upset. Longer than that can be extremely uncomfortable. So, what we like to do is ask you to reduce the alcohol intake gradually, a structured plan. To ease your body back. Do you have any questions?" Rob watches her patiently. I am interested to hear him confirm that she could be suffering hallucinations, this will explain the young visitor.

Margaret makes eye contact with Rob, then gently nods her head, "I get it." she mumbles.

Rob then takes the three of us on a guided tour, we see the place is busy, group and one to one sessions are held in small conference rooms. One group are trying pottery, another group watching an art demonstration. "We like to offer lots of alternative therapies, they are open for everyone to attend, though some are more popular than others, so you might need to book if it is a popular one." Rob concluded the tour back in his office. Margaret is positive and we talk about how the next week might be planned, with a daily reduction of cider. The support staff will bring the daily allowance on their visits. Two visits daily are planned, mid-morning and early evening.

I return to the office to draw up the plan. It is quite a big commitment, two staff a day, seven days a week. At this point I have to make staff aware of the conditions in the flat, I have already made preliminary enquiries with a cleaning company. They want access to an empty property, to deep clean and fumigate, I am not sure how I will organise this. Only one member of staff is concerned about working in these conditions, she is expecting a baby, so it is understandable.

**Sixth Visit**

It has now been three weeks since our visit to the drug and alcohol service, staff have been visiting her daily and Margaret has been following the reduced alcohol programme. Staff say she had been chatty and relaxed and appears pleased with her own progress. Today I am scheduled to make the afternoon call, I quite like the late shifts as my days seem longer, I can get more personal jobs done, like paying bills, shopping, and house cleaning.

The receptionist calls, "Hi Debbie." I answer, she has just come back from annual leave. She is the backbone of the office, knowing a little about every client and member of staff, if she isn't too busy she will help with filing and little jobs like arranging a meeting, which can take days, waiting for replies from invited staff."Good Afternoon Carla, how are you? Have not seen you in ages. Did you have a good holiday?". We spend a few minutes on catch up before Debbie divulges the reason she rang. "I had a strange call for you this morning, a Mrs Hall, said you would know who she is." The name does not ring any bells at first. "She said that she was ringing to say a big thank you because her husband George had a broken hip. He apparently had surgery two weeks ago. He is now in rehabilitation. She was really pleased and asked for you to call her." I smile realising how odd this sounds, "It's OK Debbie, I rang for the ambulance for George, that's why she phoned, I will call her back."

I feel a little smug, being right about him needing the ambulance, but also a little sad, because he had struggled for two weeks in severe pain.

Alan arrives after lunch; he has just been to visit Margaret. I enquire how she is. "Not good, when I arrived, she could not stand, I think someone has been getting her extra drink. Her speech was slurred, she was impossible to talk to. Said she hadn't been drinking, that someone called Harry had visited, an old friend?" Alan sounds frustrated.

Margaret had reduced her alcohol intake, now she had stepped backwards, she had as they say, 'fallen off the wagon' before she had found a seat, we all knew this might happen, but it was still a big disappointment. I would visit later, maybe she would be more sober then. "Did she eat anything?" I ask. "I warmed her chicken soup, she ate some." Alan confirmed. When Margaret drank, she frequently went without food, her diet was another difficult area of concern.

I arrive at Margaret's at five-thirty, the flat is in darkness and the door is closed. Fortunately, we have persuaded Margaret to have a key safe fitted, so when there is no reply, I use the key. I call out as I enter. Then I see her lying on the sofa, her head lolls off the edge, hair touching the floor. There is a stronger than usual smell of urine. An empty bottle of whiskey and two empty bottles of cider or on the floor next to her. I am not aware of Margaret drinking whiskey before? How did she get it? Maybe her mysterious visitor had brought it. I feel for a pulse, there is a faint one. Margaret does not respond when I speak to her. I call an ambulance. She is still unconscious when they leave for the hospital. I do not understand why this has happened. She was doing so well. Who is Harry?

I ring Gordon, Margaret's social worker, he is not surprised at the relapse, he had expected it to happen much sooner. I speak my thoughts aloud, "It's a pity she cannot stay in hospital for treatment, it would give us a few days, we could sort out her flat. Margaret hates hospitals so I don't think she will agree." Gordon agrees with me. I will keep him informed of her situation; I will contact the hospital tomorrow. We learn the next morning that Margaret has alcohol poisoning and could easily have died. Too much alcohol can flood the blood stream and then begin to affect parts of the brain that control vital functions like breathing, heart rate and temperature. It is unclear at this point if Margaret had a seizure or just literally passed out.

**Seventh Visit**

Gordon rings me early the next morning, he has spoken with the hospital and his Manager. Margaret is now awake, trying to leave the hospital. Staff are concerned that she may have another seizure and her blood pressure is extremely low. They want to keep her in. Gordon tells me his plan, "Can you go to the hospital and stay with her, try not to let her leave, we cannot physically restrain her."

Gordon plans to have Margaret sectioned. This means she will be kept in hospital under the Mental Health Act 1983. To section her a team of three professionals, need to assess Margaret, an approved mental health professional, a doctor (usually a psychiatrist) and a medical doctor. My role is to try and convince Margaret to stay in hospital until all three are available to do the assessment and sign the papers.

When I arrive Margaret is in bed, on the general medical ward, strategically her bed is opposite the nurse's station. I walk up to her, "Hello Margaret, how are you feeling now?" She looks at me, there is a glazed expression on her face. "Did you see that? He brought a dog in here?" She gives me a conspiratorial smile, "It's been hiding under the bed." I am not sure how to address this, so I ask, "Where is it now?" Margaret points under her bed. I look, of course there is nothing there, I ask,
"What is it called? Do you know what breed it is?" Margaret leans towards me and whispers "It's a Saint Bernard, called Rufus, be careful, he might bite."

I nod my understanding. I then talk to the imaginary dog. Suddenly, Margaret climbs off the bed and starts heading for the door, I am not allowed to physically restrain her, so I try distraction. "Margaret, I just saw Rufus run to the bed next to yours, he looks tired." Margaret looks at me, a little baffled. She starts back towards her bed, then she shouts at the top of her voice and points into the sky, "Wow look at that, can you see it wow!!" Margaret is staring out of the window, "It's a Spitfire and its heading this way." I am busily looking into the clear skies, I decide to humour her "Well, we don't see many of them over Manchester" I smile. I turn to see Margaret is hiding under her bed, with her hands over her ears. The two nurses at the station have heard my conversations and find this bizarre drama very amusing. After three hours of talking and persuading, finally, the paperwork is completed. Margaret is sectioned for assessment which can be for a period of twenty-eight days. The reason for her being sectioned is primarily the risk of her health deteriorating if she does not get treatment. Her safety is considered to be at risk, a full assessment of her mental and physical health will be undertaken.

For now, she is safe.

### Eighth Visit

I call up to the hospital to see Margaret, she has been moved to the Psychiatric Ward, I do not know what to expect. I am pleased to find the ward is modern, painted in pastel colours, with individual rooms. Each door has the patient's details on. I ring the buzzer to be admitted, the nurse lets me in and points me in the direction of her room. It is clean and calming, a soft peach colour, there is a large window overlooking the garden. The windows have bars, but not intrusive of the view. There is a small wet room with a shower, toilet, and sink. She is sitting in an armchair with her eyes closed. "Hello Margaret, remember me, Carla. How are you today?" I can see Margaret looks different, she is clean, her hair has been washed and combed and she is wearing a clean nightdress and dressing gown, given her by one of the nurses. She smiles. "I remember your face, but I do not recall your name." Margaret pulls herself upright in the chair. "Carla, Carla Saxon from social services. How are you today." She is thoughtful for a moment, then says, "Ah yes I remember you brought the chicken sandwich and crisps." I nod. "How are you?" She looks at me and says, "I am lonely, I hardly see anyone. I am sad because I know why I have been admitted in here, I want to go home." Margaret stares out of the window. I realise how quiet and peaceful it is, no hustle and bustle of staff and visitors, the place is perfect for meditation and reflection.

We both sit looking at the garden and I recall some twenty years earlier, still in college, studying 'A levels' at the tender age of twenty-three. I contemplated becoming a psychiatric nurse. To this end, my weekends were spent as a volunteer, visiting some of the large psychiatric hospitals in Greater London. Many of these hospitals were the original asylums built in the early eighteen hundreds. One in particular I remember stood in its own grounds, away from the city, away from the general public. A high wall surrounded the premises. The property had large gardens with trees and shrubs. The building was in true Victorian, Gothic style. Dark stone with a grand entrance, a large wooden door, columns on either side. Despite its grandeur there was a sinister feel about it, maybe it was just the images the word 'asylum' conjures. The windows were tall and dark, with bars. We were a group of five volunteers, escorted by a senior member of staff. Primarily we are there to visit patients who had no family or friends. We were given a little snippet of the hospital's history, as we walked through the entrance hall. Years ago, many people were admitted not for mental health issues but because they were a social embarrassment to their family, a speech impediment or deafness being two common examples. We were introduced to a lovely lady of ninety-two years, she had been admitted when she was four, because she could not speak and was profoundly deaf, she had been judged as 'clumsy' and 'stupid', her family abandoned her. Several years later attempts were made to re-introduce her into society, but as she was already institutionalised. It was deemed unsafe for her to be on her own in the world. Her speech was still limited, but her general persona was happy and cheerful.

We were escorted through two consecutive locked gated doorways, into a corridor with rooms off on each side, the rooms all had metal, lockable doors much like prison cells. At the end of the corridor was a larger room full of women, all different ages, the room was eerily silent, the women moved around in the isolated worlds of their own minds. Several of them came over to us, curiously staring and touching us. We spoke to them, but they did not hear. One woman stroked my arm, I felt shivers down my back, she was staring at me, but her eyes were absent.

I attended these visiting sessions for several weeks, I was befriended by two gentleman, they had a condition which we now refer to as Downs-Syndrome. Each week they waited in the grounds for my arrival, hugged me and escorted me into the building They loved to chatter. One week the psychiatrist asked me if I would consider visiting the children's section, I agreed, I was introduced to a number of adolescents, moving around in a shared space. Many of them were in wheelchairs and the majority wore helmets to prevent injury from shaking or banging their heads. It struck me that this environment was probably the same as it had been a hundred years ago.

Then one week I was asked if I would like to meet a

long-term resident, whom the staff found extremely difficult to interact with. My curiosity aroused I followed the psychiatrist. The room was the size of a school dining hall, there were however, no tables or chairs it was empty. Windows lined the top of the walls, too high to see through, the walls were covered in dark green tiles. Then I saw him. The psychiatrist squeezed my arm, "Are you OK?" He asked. I nodded. The doctor walked over to the small childlike figure stood in the corner of the room. Slowly he turned the naked figure to face me. At that point, my heart leapt, mixed emotions I did not know how to process, fear, horror, panic, sorrow, compassion, pity. What I had thought was a twelve-year old boy was actually a twenty-one-year old man. Abandoned at birth. This was Johnathon.

His tiny frail body, childlike and so thin his bones were protruding through his skin - his face. Should I run in fear or hug him with love? Never could I have ever imagined a face so disfigured. Every feature had shifted; he was difficult to recognise as a human being. He was naked because his skin was so sensitive that he could not bear to have anything touch it. Johnathon was unable to hear, speak or see. Day after day staff tried ways to communicate, each effort had failed. "If you can offer any suggestions or ideas, we will be pleased to try them." The doctor looked at me. I had nothing to offer. Johnathon spent his days and nights trapped in his body, trapped in a world without meaning. His movements consisted of standing, sitting, lying, and rubbing his stomach. He rubbed his stomach frequently, no one knew why, was he in pain? Did it give him comfort? Or was it a reflex action?

When we left that day, I knew my life had been changed forever. I was plagued by nightmares; I could not remove the image of Johnathon from my mind. I no longer felt able to work as a psychiatric nurse. I was tortured for weeks with thoughts of this soul, this lost soul in constant torment. I never visited again.

Margaret is staying in a much better place; times have changed for the better. She looks brighter, her eyes have lost their dullness, her skin looks better - a slight colour in her cheeks. She turns and smiles at me. "Do you see the squirrels in that far tree, they are so busy each day, collecting nuts and storing them. Bit like this place eh?" Margaret grins at me. "You are not 'nuts' Margaret! You are a lovely lady who just got taken in by a controlling man. Don't be so hard on yourself. You are a very brave lady to have got this far." I mean every word I say. We then have a coffee together, she talks freely, "You know it's hard to describe what it feels like when I want a drink, my body craves alcohol. It is like being in a desert and needing water, every nerve in my body needs alcohol, every thought in my head is focused on the next drink. It takes over, nothing else matters. At first, I drank to get drunk, to feel better. Then it was drinking to feel normal. I hate myself for not being stronger." Margaret sighs.

I try to cheer the mood, I ask her how she will feel if we get the flat cleaned up ready for her return, get the toilet and the cooker fixed. Margaret says that would be great, she is not looking forward to going home to the mess. I ask about Michelle, "When did you last have contact with your daughter?" She looks to the window again, "Be about ten or fifteen years ago, when I was staying in the first hostel. I got moved to another hostel and spent a year on the streets after that. Not really good at being homeless," she smiles. "I like my bed too much and anyway the methylated spirits did not agree with me. I finished up in one of these places. I have not heard from Michelle for years. Although an old friend Harry visited me last week, he said Michelle lives in a small village about five miles away, she is married now and has two children. Me, a grandmother, I can't imagine that." Margaret looks sad, something else she had lost.

I am curious about Harry, I ask, "Did Harry buy you the whiskey?" "No. No Harry is strictly a teetotaller; he gave me thirty pounds to get some food. I guess I felt so low, I thought I deserved a decent drink." Margaret had a real reason for slipping back, it must have been hard to learn she had a family nearby. Harry was a colleague she worked with before she met David. He always had a soft spot for her, he never married. "He is still in the profession. He works with adolescents in London; he is up here visiting his mother". Margaret stares through the window, possibly remembering happier days. I ask, "How did he find you?" "He knew my married name, he also knew I had moved into this area, found me on the electoral register, strange that because I do not recall registering. Anyway, one of the neighbours told him I was in hospital."

That evening Paul and I go to the cinema, it is a comedy, we both enjoy the light relief. After we call and buy a fish and chip supper. Paul spends the night, Mr. Tom is a little jealous and I wake up to find him lying between us in the bed, I stroke him, he jumps down and starts to meow for breakfast.

Time to get up.

**Ninth Visit**

Before I go to the hospital, I decide to call in to see how the cleaning company are getting along. The only thing Margaret has asked, is that a carpet rolled up in the bedroom be kept, she thought it could be fitted somewhere else. The van is outside, I can hear movement on the stairs, Jim appears carrying one end of a roll of carpet the other end is supported by his wife. They own the cleaning company. He greets me like a long-lost friend, without the hugs. I ask them, "Is the carpet out of the bedroom, because she wants to keep it." They both look at me, then at the carpet on the concrete. "Do not think she will want to keep this." Jim says as he raises his foot and brings it down hard on the carpet. Hundreds of maggots, beetles, moths, flies, earwigs, and a number of spiders run from within the carpet roll. I let out an involuntary scream, "No, I think it had better go, I will explain to her." They both nod, pick up the carpet and throw it into the van. Most of the furniture has gone to the city dump now. Jim informs me the fumigation will take place over night, then tomorrow the cleaning team will move in. "Great, thank you Jim." I am pleased I opted for this company.

Jim smiles and adds "By the way I think you win our top award." I look confused. "You see we have deep cleaned over five hundred houses in this town. But you found us the dirtiest one we have ever seen." I laugh. "I know you like a challenge." With that I make my exit.

Margaret is just finishing her lunch as I arrive, some sort of pasta bake. I can see that her weight is improving, she has been eating regular meals now for over two weeks. She feels the medication she is taking makes her hungry. I see she has a magazine and has been doing the crossword. "I didn't know you liked crosswords, Margaret." She glances at the magazine, "Oh yes, I used to do the Times crossword every day in my lunch break, when I was working." I suddenly catch a glimpse of the Margaret that was, smart, confident, intelligent, and attractive. We chat about her work as a child psychologist, she is truly knowledgeable on her subject. She loves children, which is why she wanted a career working with them. Suddenly she asks, "Do you think I could find Daniel?" I was not sure how to answer her, so decide on a straight answer. "I think if you can get a hold on the alcohol issues, get your life back on track, then it should be possible to find him and maybe build a relationship. You need to conquer one mountain at a time." Margaret smiles, "so how is my flat doing?"

"Ah, well on that subject. I am afraid the rolled-up carpet in the bedroom was beyond redemption, completely ruined by wildlife. The sofa was pretty bad too. We are going to try and sort something out before you come home next week. Alan and Shirley are working on that as we speak." She reaches over and takes my hand, "I am really grateful, and I am going to give this my best shot." As I leave, I genuinely believe Margaret has turned a corner.

Back at the office, Alan and Shirley are in great form, the banter and laughter around the office is contagious. Shirley explains that they have been to the Salvation Army's Furniture warehouse and purchased, in Shirley's words, "A unique, designer sofa and matching chair, in brown leather' for Margaret. I would have taken it for my house if Margaret were not in greater need." Shirley announces. The deal is that a person 'in need' can purchase seven items of furniture for a set price of forty pounds. Initially, this was to help the homeless setting up a new home.

Shirley had never been before she is excited by her discoveries. "I could not believe it; they have three floors of furniture. Everything, beds, wardrobes, tables, chairs really Carla, it is like an Aladdin's Cave! "

When the joviality has quietened down, I say to Alan. "It is a shame we cannot get the place decorated; Margaret does not have enough funds from the grant we got." Alan looks at me, "Does she have enough money for paint? Cause if she does, I don't mind going in and giving the place a coat of emulsion." I am not surprised by Alan's kind gesture. "Yes, she has, if you are willing, then I will help too, I am sure Paul will give us a couple of hours also." I grin. Shirley, Adrian, Mike and even Gordon volunteer their time. Most of the team offer but we decide it is best not to have too many people in a small flat.

That evening Paul and I call and collect the necessary materials for the decorating. Paul is enthusiastic, everyone likes Margaret and wants her to succeed. If decorating her flat helps her do that then we will do it. Strictly speaking it is not on our job description, which is why we are doing this in our own time.

**Tenth Visit**

Last week we spent our free time, before and after shifts, painting the flat. Margaret had said she liked cream, so the living room is cream with white paintwork. We had some paint left, so the hallway was given a coat too. The toilet was fixed, a second-hand cooker has been purchased and fitted. The living room smells fresh and clean, the second-hand designer leather sofa sits in the middle. We all enjoy the teamwork, a common cause, we all feel a sense of pride in our efforts, and we cannot wait to see Margaret's reaction.

I collect Margaret from the hospital, she is quiet, nervous. I wondered if she is worried about her flat. She has money for the week, so staff have bought her some basic food stuff. Margaret does not speak on the way back; she has not had a drink for four weeks. She has medication to counteract the withdrawal symptoms. A drug called acamprosate has been prescribed to help her stay off the alcohol, the sessions will continue with the drug and alcohol services. Plus, our team will provide daily support.

When we arrive at the flat Shirley is waiting for us, Margaret is still looking scared, she is unsure. I encourage her, I talk about how everyone helped, everyone sends their best wishes. She goes into the flat first. Shirley and I hang back, it feels like we are on one of the TV programmes where families have a make-over of their homes. We follow her inside. Margaret is standing in the room, staring at the window. We wait, two minutes, three minutes then she turns around. "I don't deserve this, if it weren't for you lot, your team, I would be dead now. Why have you done this for me? I really don't deserve all this." With that a single tear rolled down her cheek. We both move forward and hug her. I say, "You do deserve this and a lot more, you deserve to be well, to be happy, to have friends." She begins to sob, "Thank you so much, thank you."

Margaret did not have a drink for six months, she then relapsed. With support she started the programme again, three times she relapsed, three times she fought back. Margaret did not have alcohol for three years. She found Daniel and he now visits her regularly with his son. Michelle has telephoned her, maybe one day they will meet again.

Everyone needs someone to care. In Margaret's case she had an entire team.

# Chapter Three
# Stephen

'Everything you can imagine is real.'

Pablo Picasso

**First Visit**

It is not possible to like every client, I tell myself. I do not need to like them to work with them, to care for them. Sometimes however, it is a struggle. I arrive at the house feeling a little nervous, we have never worked with this client before. The young man has lived alone for two years, in the community. Supported by his family and the Mental Health Team, his father lived with him; two older brothers live nearby. Now his father has met a new partner. He decided, after twenty-nine years of caring for his son, it was time to get a life. He moved to Spain.

Social Services first heard of Stephen's plight yesterday, when his father rang from Spain, saying he was unable to contact his son. The social worker who took the call soon realised that there was a problem, as information unfolded, Stephen's vulnerability became clear. She rang the doctor and psychiatrist, who had both been involved with Stephen over the years. He would require help immediately. He had been alone for twenty-four hours.

So here I am waiting outside the house for the social worker, Lorrie, to arrive. Lorrie is a very competent senior social worker, very skilled at her job. I like the way she works, direct and to the point - says what she needs from us. However, I am also aware that she can be ruthless and extremely ambitious. Noticeably young for her age, at forty-two she could easily be mistaken for a twenty-something year old. Her short pixie cut hairstyle and smart, severe style of dress give her an air of authority. Lorrie arrives on time and we walk together to the door.

This is a social housing estate but many of the properties are now owned by the tenants. You can see at a glance which ones are no longer rented. The first thing people tend to do when they purchase their council house is change the front door. This house has a different front door. The house belongs to Stephen's father. Lorrie knocks.

"His father said he has been trying to ring him, Stephen is not answering." Lorrie says as she discovers a bell and presses it.

"I just want to do a preliminary assessment; see how big a problem we have." Lorrie raises the letterbox flap to peer inside, just as the door opens. Standing in the doorway is a handsome young man, short dark hair, soft green eyes, he is staring at us with a blank expression. Dressed in jogging pants and a tee shirt, his feet are bare. "Stephen?" Lorrie asks, he nods his head.

"Hello, my name is Lorrie, and this is Carla, your Dad asked us to call in, to make sure you are OK. Can we come in please?" Stephen still appears confused, he turns and goes back into the house, we follow.

The house is well presented, clean with modern furnishings. There is a large LED TV screen covering the wall over the fireplace, opposite is a settee with a game controller on the armrest, this is obviously where Stephen was sitting. Lorrie asks if we might sit down, he nods, we both opt for armchairs. "Stephen, how are you managing without your Dad here? Are you getting enough to eat?" Lorrie asks. Stephen is holding the controller and staring at the screen, he nods.

"Stephen, can I ask you to switch that off please, just for a few minutes while we have a chat?" Lorrie says as she takes out her notebook and pen. He looks at Lorrie, as though slowly processing this request, then switches the game off. The TV is still switched on, the screen is scratchy now, as if the aerial has been disconnected. Lorrie asks, "Could you turn the sound down please?" He obeys. "Thank you. Have you eaten today?" he nods. "What did you have?" Stephen stands up, goes into the kitchen. He brings back an empty microwave burger box, potato fries packet, an empty yoghurt pot and several wrappers from bars of chocolate. Lorrie is busily making notes. I ask, "Do you like burgers Stephen?" He nods. I am starting to wonder if he can actually speak. As Lorrie continues writing, he stares blankly at the screen.

Suddenly, he shouts, looking frantically from Lorrie to me, "Did you see that, did you see it?" We are both confused, "See what?" We ask in unison. "The message, the coded message." Lorrie and I exchange glances. "Did you see it; they have been sending them all night." Stephen is excited, anxious for us to say something.
"Sorry Stephen, didn't see anything, where did you see it?" Lorrie asks. "In the corner of the screen, its coded, I have been trying to work out the code". He passes me a piece of paper with random detailed drawings on, if he has drawn these, they are excellent. "Who is sending the messages?" Lorrie enquires as she continues to write things down. "Aliens, they are coming, some of them are already here." He watches the screen intently and begins scribbling on a piece of paper. Lorrie leaves the room saying, "Alright if I use your bathroom Stephen?" He does not notice she has gone. I know she is checking the other rooms.

Then Stephen stands up, still staring directly ahead, he starts to walk around the room. He is following a pattern through the furniture, silent, staring trance-like directly ahead. I try to engage with him, "Is everything alright, do you need something?" He does not hear. He walks round and round in a figure of eight. When he reaches the point behind my chair he stops. I can hear his breathing, he is extremely close, my personal body space is being invaded. He mutters something, then continues on his circuit of the room. I attempt to speak to him again, he either does not hear me or is deliberately ignoring me.

He is now muttering, whispering continually, I cannot understand him. He is moving around the same circuit, walking faster and faster. He disappears out of the room, I can here Lorrie upstairs, he is still mumbling. He comes back into the room and opens a large cupboard under the staircase, peering inside. Suddenly, he makes a loud, long high shrill scream. I jump up, I am shaking. Hell! what was that? I am shocked into silence. Lorrie rushes in, sees Stephen, then gently says "Come on Stephen, take a seat, can I get you something to drink?" He looks at Lorrie, slowly as though he has just woken up, returns to his seat and asks for a coffee. Still in shock, I feel the need for a double brandy.

I go to the kitchen to make coffee, I can hear Lorrie talking calmly, "Stephen, did your Dad get you all the food in the kitchen?" Stephen replies "No a man comes with a big green van, every Thursday, brings lots of stuff." We quickly assess that his father arranges an online shop each week. Which means he has no reason to go out. His father has informed Lorrie that he is not coming back to the UK for a year. Stephen will definitely need support during this time. He drinks his coffee; Lorrie asks what he will eat later, he replies. "Hot-dogs and ice cream." Lorrie then asks if Stephen would like someone to come and see him each day, to make sure he is alright. "Yeah, that's OK. After ten o clock because I like to sleep in. Can I put my game on now?" Lorrie thanks Stephen for talking to us and tells him he can go back to his game. We let ourselves out.

Outside Lorrie explains there is not a lot we can do at this stage, he is not at risk, he is not in danger, he is caring for himself, his kitchen is clean and tidy, his bedroom is a bit untidy but his bed has been made. The house was the family home, Stephen is comfortable and familiar with his surroundings. His brother will continue to support him one day a week. Lorrie will send me a detailed plan of the support required, by tomorrow. Along with reports regarding Stephen's history and mental health. We each go our separate ways, I am not sure about Stephen, there is something unpredictable about him, something quite scary.

That evening I decide to do some homework, I have assumed that Stephen may suffer from psychosis, it will be confirmed when I receive the file. I do not understand psychosis, if indeed this is his condition. After a delicious supper of chilli-con-carne, made by Paul, who has developed a love of cooking. I go on my computer to do some research. Paul is watching the football.

Psychosis is a condition of the mind which results in the person being unable to determine what is real and what is not. Stephen appears to be spending a lot of time on his computer games, maybe this would increase his inability to separate fantasy from reality? People with this condition often hallucinate, hear, and see things that others cannot, Stephen's belief that he saw a message on the TV screen would be a good example. Psychotic disorders can include Schizophrenia or Bipolar symptoms. I am not clear why Stephen was wandering in a set pattern or why he suddenly screamed, I read a few case studies, but it is not clear.

The working of the human mind has always fascinated me, I studied psychology at college, I found it gave me an insight into human behaviour. During this period, I met a man called Phillip, he lived in an institution. His hobby was jigsaw puzzles, he had completed hundreds of them. The thing was he never looked at the picture, he completed the puzzles based purely upon the shape of the pieces. He would deliberately turn the picture side over because the colours confused him. He needed only the shapes. Phillip was also a terrific artist, he could see a face for a few seconds, and could then produce a pencil portrait, an exact likeness of the person. Stephen has creative skills, the drawings he showed me were intricate diagrams of machinery and mechanical workings, no doubt in some way related to his 'coded messages'. The mind is a marvellous machine but possibly dangerous when it malfunctions.

Paul interrupts my train of thought with a coffee, it's half time, his team are losing. "Think I will have this coffee with you then head home, got an early start tomorrow." Paul is off to Liverpool for training, I have heard about this course, it has a particularly good reputation. The subject is, 'dealing with difficult and challenging behaviour.' I am hoping I get the opportunity to attend at some point, it's organised by a private company, especially for staff working in the community. There is a long waiting list for places. We have our goodnight kiss and Paul leaves. I decide to have a quick shower and go to bed.

**Second Visit**

It was all over the news this morning, local man stabbed to death in dispute over drugs. The body of Joseph Swan aged forty-seven was discovered yesterday morning in his home in Higher Thornton. He had been stabbed several times, a neighbour reported seeing a 'suspicious' person loitering around the flat earlier in the day. Joseph had no family members. He was currently under the care of mental health and social services.

I am shocked when I hear the news, this was 'James

Bond' the client I had met some months previously, Tony was his social worker. The report continued, A friend said, "Joseph was a kind and generous man, he had some medical issues and was also receiving treatment for his personality disorder.' James Bond' is how I will always remember him; he was so convincing. He believed he was a secret agent. We all knew he was harmless but extremely vulnerable. All too often the vulnerable in society are abused by unscrupulous people, usually for financial gain. Frequently their stories have an unhappy ending.

Today I am here to support Stephen preparing lunch. Initially, this is a familiarisation process, to assess what he is able to do and which areas he needs support with. I arrive at the house at twelve-fifteen. Stephen answers the door. I can see he does not remember who I am.

"Hello Stephen, I am Carla, I came to see you yesterday with Lorrie. Do you remember me?" I watch for a reaction, his face is without expression, he replies, "Yes." Then turns and retreats back into the house. I follow him in, I am still nervous and hope this does not show.

"I have come to help you to prepare some lunch, what would you like to eat today?" I watch as Stephen sits on the sofa staring straight ahead.

I try to talk about things which may interest him, many topics fall on stony ground, like football, rugby, sports in general, reading, TV. The topics draw no response. "What about music Stephen, what sort of music do you like?" Stephen stands up and goes to a small cupboard, he removes several CDs, which he passes to me. I am incredibly surprised to see they are all sixties music, "You like sixties music?" I smile, having finally found a shared interest. Stephen sits back on the sofa. "Yes, my dad and my brother like sixties music too. I like T Rex, The Kinks, the Beatles and of course the Rolling Stones. Do you like David Bowie?" Stephen for the first time is having a proper adult conversation, I feel more relaxed. He says the CD collection is his, he likes to buy CDs from the sixties, he also has a book 'Music of the Sixties', which he brings for me to read. We chat for about twenty minutes, then I return to the topic of food. "So, Stephen, shall we go and see what you can have for lunch?"

I stand up to move into the kitchen, Stephen also stands. Once in the kitchen he washes his hands, I find some baking potatoes. "Would you like a baked potato? We can cook it in the microwave?" Stephen turns to look at me and nods, then continues to wash his hands. I find some butter, cheese, and a tin of beans. I wait, he continues to wash his hands, each finger is washed, between each finger, he methodically soaps then rinses his hands, over and over. I wait. I feel I need to distract him. "Stephen would you like to set the table and I will get your potato ready." He looks at me and nods. Three minutes later Stephen starts to dry his hands. Another five minutes passes, the potato is in the microwave and the beans in a pan on a low heat. Stephen sets the table. Once the food is ready, I place it on a plate and put it on the table, he is already sitting quietly, waiting. I decide it's best to leave him to eat on his own, I tell him I will wait in the living room. Twenty minutes later I hear movement, the tap is running, I peep into the kitchen. He is washing up and tidying everything away. I sit and wait.

Stephen returns to the living room, with an absent look on his face. I am sitting in the armchair. He starts to walk the circuit he has walked the previous day. Silently. He moves around, staring straight ahead. He walks behind me, should I turn? I cannot see what he is doing, then I hear he is in the kitchen, then back in the room with me, so close behind me the hairs on the back of my neck begin to prickle. He extends the circuit and goes faster, still no sound comes from him; he goes up the stairs. I am unsure what to do. He is marching loudly across the bedroom floor, I can hear other sounds, not words, more like small animal sounds. Then he is back downstairs, he goes to the cupboard under the stairs. Even though I am half expecting him to do it, when he lets out the long shrill scream into the dark cupboard, every nerve in my body is on edge, I want to run. Stephen turns and comes to sit on the sofa, "Is it OK for me to play my game now?" he asks. I nod. "Yes, I have to be going, is there anything you need before tomorrow?" He is no longer here, he is in his game.

I am so relieved to be out of the house, I climb quickly into my car and lock the doors. This is irrational I tell myself, why are you worrying about him? There is definitely something odd, frightening about this handsome young man. The way he stares at me, intensely, as though he is trying to see inside me. I give an involuntary shiver.

It is extremely busy back in the office, there are no computers available. I have my laptop; I still need a seat. Bill sees me and calls me into his office. "Glad I caught you, I wanted to have a word." Bill has obviously eaten his lunch, there is an empty plate on his desk, along with wrappers from various confections. He sits himself down.
"How are things going? "Bill asks. It is not time for my supervision meeting, so I wonder why he asks. My confusion must show. "Just a general question, no hidden agenda," he adds. "Things are OK, But, well this new client, Stephen. I am not sure about him. I think we should be working in pairs with him, I am finding him a bit 'creepy'. I explain. "Creepy, well that's a new

term for our clients." He says smiling. "No honestly, there is something unpredictable about him. I think we need to review any risk assessments for this man." I am speaking out again, my soap box is in use. Bill listens intently, as I describe the support session.

Bill then says. "You know what, I believe I know Stephen, is it Stephen Matthews, lives on Wild Brook Road?" I nod. "It's a few years ago now but I remember him, he was at school when I met him. Stephen had persistent thoughts that Aliens were trying to get in touch with him, he talked about coded messages, signals they were sending. At one point he claimed the school computers were all infected by an Alien virus which was causing malfunctions in other electronic areas, if a light bulb went or someone left a computer on in error, these things were signs of the 'alien' presence. His anxiety levels at school became so high that his overall performance was affected, he went from a grade A student to a D. Stephen's friends started to notice his comments and odd behaviour, slowly he became isolated, he was definitely considered different. Yes, I remember now, He developed a tendency to scream or howl, abruptly without warning, these sounds were often followed by extreme anger and aggressive behaviour. Sometimes he would stop speaking mid-sentence, like someone had flicked a switch, he would be in a trance-like state for several seconds. Or he would stare into the distance as though he could see or hear something. In the end his parents had to remove him from school, he was being bullied by some pupils, also lots of his peers were fearful of his unusual behaviour and temper. He believed that everyday electronics, like phones, TV sets, radios even electric cookers were tools used by aliens to plan an invasion of Earth.
I always felt a little sad for Stephen, he was the youngest of three brothers, a gentle frail youngster, afraid of his own shadow." Bill

gathers the paper wrappers from his desk, deep in thought, he throws them in the waste-paper basket.

I feel a little guilty now, have I let my own fear and prejudice, cloud my judgment, this is someone's son, he has brothers, parents, grandparents. He has a condition, not all conditions are easily loved. I tell myself I must try harder.
"Sorry Bill, what was it you wanted to see me about." Bill gets up and closes the door. "Ah yes, this is strictly confidential for now. It's about the department." Bill explains that there are changes being discussed regarding the team structure, an amalgamation of our team with another team is being considered. If this goes ahead another manager will be needed to work alongside Bill.
"It would be an exceptionally large team, covering a big area, with a much wider range of clients. Are there plans to relocate?" I am always wary of teams being too big, if there are too many people, control, comradeship, motivation, and supervision become more difficult. Not to mention the considerable lack of space at present. The other team currently operate from an outpost on the other side of town, which could mean long journeys for staff. "Plans are to reduce the number of staff, some will be redeployed to other areas. There are other premises available. The reason I am telling you this is because I would like you to consider applying for the position of manager." Bill leans back in his chair and grins. I am surprised, I am not sure if I want to move into a managerial role again. I have a really good relationship with my colleagues, how will they take it if I become their manager?

My mind goes back over twenty-five years, I worked in a factory producing potato crisps, my role was machine operator, packing the products. I liked the job, it was easy. It was also boring. They advertised for a night foreman, at twenty-one no task was too daunting, I could do it. I applied and got an interview. At the interview I felt I did not have the skills they required, however, I was able to offer my views on how production could be improved, why staff needed to be better trained and how the system of recording needed to be redesigned. The next day Mr Beech the manager sent for me, he told me I had not been successful. I took it on the chin, I had been expecting a rejection.

As I thanked him and stood to leave, he said, "However, we were very impressed with your interview." I smiled "Thanks." He then continued "We have another job which we feel is more suited to you, how would you feel about being a training officer." I was surprised; this was definitely a step up from machine operator and foreman. Of course, I accepted.

The following week I exchanged my blue overall for a pristine white coat. Most of my first few days were spent in the office, learning the ropes, I was very keen. By Friday I missed the banter and gossip with the women on the line, so at lunch time I went to join them in the canteen. I bought my lunch and joined a group at the middle table. Suddenly the conversation stopped. I asked if everyone was alright, a couple of women nodded. Within five minutes I found everyone had gone, except for an older lady who had worked in the same job for years. "Was it something I said?" I laughed. She looked at me and said, "You are management now, not one of us. You need to eat with the bosses." With that she smiled, collected her tray, and left. I suppose it was my first lesson in management, it is not possible to wear both hats. I knew I would be a good, fair training officer, I just needed time to learn and earn respect.

I tell Bill I appreciate his offer and I am grateful for his support; I just need a couple of days to think about it. Bill says, "If you are worried how your colleagues will react, they will give you their full support. Give it some serious thought." I sometimes think Bill knows me too well.

Paul meets me after work, and we go to a local restaurant for a meal. The place is not too crowded, it is a carvery, or you can order from a menu, we find a seat and order. We laugh as we select, chatting about life, crazy diets, and general trivia. Then Paul says, "I have something I need to tell you." I look at him puzzled, I have never seen him look so serious, "What is it, I hate surprises?" Paul picks up his glass of wine, "I have been offered another job, a better job." I laugh. "No! So, have I. What have you been offered? Wow, that's unbelievable, both on the same day!"

Paul still looks serious. "Actually, I was offered the job last month, I have been considering my options. Its twice the salary I am on now, less hours, definitely a step up the professional ladder." I look at him, whilst he is smiling, his eyes look sad. "So, if it's that great why haven't you accepted?" Paul looks serious again, "I have!" "Oh, well that is great, we should be celebrating. When do you start, which organisation is it?" Paul hesitates, "Actually, it is in New Zealand and I start in two weeks."

I do what I always do when confronted with something hurtful, I put on my stiff upper lip, try to remain calm and under no circumstances must the person hurting me detect how I feel. "Oh, well that is quick, I am incredibly pleased for you. It sounds like an excellent opportunity. So, I assume you will be moving out there, permanently?" I am hoping he was going to say something romantic, impulsive. He just nods. "They have sorted accommodation for me." The evening did not go well after that, I feigned interest and he tried not to sound too enthusiastic. It ended abruptly after the main course, I said I had a migraine, I never actually told him my news. We kissed goodbye in the car park.

That night Mr Tom was my only comfort. I was sad but somehow stoical, my track record with romance is not good. Whenever I feel close to someone the world always comes crashing down. After Martin died, I grieved for six months, then friends encouraged me to 'get out there', 'you are still young', plenty of opportunities'. I went out there, joined classes and groups, my life became full of social activities. I never met anyone. Maybe I was still giving off the grieving widow signals. They say bad things happen in threes, later I had three disastrous relationships and decided I was better off single. Now I have my fourth.

**Third Visit**

I have not seen Bill for three days, this morning he is in early. I tell him I would like to apply for the job. He actually hugs me, which I find a little disconcerting, a bit like being hugged by your best friend's boyfriend - awkward. He is obviously pleased.

Other staff have been visiting Stephen. Alan and Adrian report back that everything is fine, though they do privately admit to me, they find Stephen's behaviour a little weird. Shirley confides that she feels threatened, even though Stephen has not actually done anything wrong. We have not received any risk assessments and have only a limited amount of information about him, no background details as yet. I sent an email to Lorrie requesting access to his full file and risk assessments. Lorrie did not get back to me. I feel very strongly that we should not be working with someone, until we receive all the information. So I rang Lorrie yesterday afternoon and explained these concerns, she replied, "You are given information on a need to know basis, I will forward details later today. I have been terribly busy; I am still here after a night-shift." I did not consider her response helpful.

I arrive at Stephen's at twelve-fifteen, the specified time, he opens the door on the third ring. Today Stephen looks different, his hair is ruffled, he still has his pyjama pants on with a tee-shirt. I follow him through to the living room. "Good morning Stephen, how are you today?" He takes a few moments to respond, "They were here last night sending messages. I did not sleep. Do you know what they are planning?" I am not sure how to respond, "No, what are they planning?" I ask. Stephen looks directly at me, "They are taking over human forms, they will be everywhere soon." At this point I feel it might be better to talk about normal things. "Are you hungry? What do you feel like eating?" I wait for a reply. Several seconds pass then Stephen says, "Burger".

I stand to go into the kitchen and Stephen robotically follows me. He commences the ritual of washing his hands, I watch as he scrubs them using a small sponge, the type used for washing up dishes, with an abrasive pad on one side. He scrubs each finger. And constantly passes his hands under the tap. I find the Burgers and some rolls; I defrost the roll in the microwave and place the burger in a pan. Stephen continues to wash his hands. I am considering using a distraction when suddenly he stops, wipes his hands, and disappears into the hallway, I hear him climbing the stairs. The bathroom is upstairs, I assume that is where he has gone.

A loud, protracted howl, sounding like a wild beast in extreme pain, echoes around the house. My blood runs cold, I am seized with an intense fear. Another screeching howl followed by another. I am on automatic pilot, I switch the cooker off, place the pan and plates to the back of the worktop. I can hear the howling, then silence. I move forward towards the front of the house. Then I hear something being dragged across the floor, followed by an explosion of sound, as whatever it is comes tumbling down the stairs, I hear the shrill sound of glass breaking. My legs are frozen to the spot, somewhere in my head I decide I need to grab my phone, it is in my bag, in the living room. I move forward and clasp my bag. I hear Stephen coming down the stairs, he is shouting and ranting a stream of obscenities. I am shaking so much I cannot find my phone. I see Stephen pass the doorway and charge into the kitchen. He is still yelling, now he is literally smashing the kitchen furniture, I can here chairs breaking as they are thrown against the wall. I have my phone; my fingers are shaking so much I cannot operate it. Then the howling reaches a crescendo, suddenly Stephen is there, face to face with me. He is staring at me, but he is not seeing me, he is not Stephen, he is a wild animal, consumed with rage. Stephen towers over me, I feel tiny, I am trembling, my mouth is dry, my heart is pounding. He starts to direct his words at me, they make no sense, they are interspersed with foul language "Argonian, Fuck Devil Jen, Shit Drell, Drow, Pissed Gerudo." He screams the words directly at me.

I am a statue, nowhere to go, frozen in time. Then Stephen picks up a waste paper basket and throws it in my direction, he misses. He turns, opens the front door, and runs out. I can hear him screaming in the street. I run and close the door. I ring the office, Bill speaks calmly, "Are you alright, did he hurt you? Yes, it is OK to close the door, you must ensure you are safe." He tells me to wait, he will be there in five minutes, five minutes can feel like hours. What if Stephen comes back?

When Bill arrives, he is practical and organised. Lorrie has been informed and she will contact Stephen's brother. At this stage she does not feel the police need to be involved. Forty-five minutes later Stephen is returned to the house, by his older brother. His brother comes into the living room and tells Stephen to go upstairs and get changed. He is filthy, I have no idea where he has been. Bill and I clear the broken mirror from the bottom of the stairs and put back the kitchen chairs, two broken ones are stacked in the rear passageway. His brother I learn is Harold, an older version of Stephen, same short haircut, and soft eyes. He goes into the kitchen. "What a mess eh? Do you know what triggered his outburst?" he is asking me. I reply, thinking there is no trigger, "I have absolutely no idea.".

Harold goes to the sink and starts to wash his hands, I see a mirror of the same ritual being performed, scrubbing each finger, concentrating, over and over. The kettle switches off, Harold stops to make tea. Stephen comes back down; he is wearing clean pyjamas. He looks exhausted, his eyes are downcast, he now appears like a small child, frightened, lost and confused. Harold passes him a mug, instructing him to drink, then to go for a lie down and try to get some sleep. Harold says he will stay with his brother for the rest of the afternoon. We have staff scheduled to return for the evening call, He cancels their visit.

I feel traumatised by the experience, Bill can see I am upset and tells me to go home. We can debrief in the morning. He will arrange a meeting with Lorrie and the staff rostered to support Stephen.

This evening I am more shaken than I care to admit, I have never felt so vulnerable, so exposed to danger, in my life. What was I doing? Why was I placing myself at risk like this? I imagine what Martin, my late husband, would have said, "I will murder this Stephen", "I insist that you change jobs", he would have reasoned that with my history, I was stupid to risk my life. I think what Paul might say, I feel, he would probably just accept the incident, as a risk which goes with the job. Did I want to accept such a risk? Paul does not know my history, I do not go around wearing a badge, or looking for sympathy. I am now healthier than I have ever been in my life. Still, I should not take my gift for granted, I sometimes forget how lucky I have been.

My faulty heart was first diagnosed when I was thirty-one. After that there were hospital appointments, tests, and numerous trials of medications. I had learned as a child how to live with my illness, but everything wears out with age, my heart deteriorated. Cardiomyopathy or in layman's terms, 'Sudden death Syndrome' was a cross that my family had to bear. As the years went by, I was given various medications, which had side effects. I dealt with these in my stride, turning blue, shaking, migraines and dizziness. Over a seven-year period I was hospitalised twenty-three times as an emergency, Blue flashing lights to add to the drama.

The final couple of years I was so poorly; breathing became extremely difficult, any form of physical activity was exhausting. Some days, cleaning my teeth would leave me so fatigued I needed to lie down and rest for several minutes. If I wanted to go out a wheelchair was used. I did not know when my heart would decide to go into atrial fibrillation, I just knew when it had. Sometimes I was unable to lift my head off the pillow, my blood pressure would fall dramatically. The disease cardiomyopathy carries a higher risk in children when the heart is still developing. The heart muscle thickens over time, so becomes less efficient at circulating blood. In children, exercise can cause the heart to be pushed beyond its capacity, it cannot keep up the flow of blood to other organs and muscles, the rhythm becomes erratic. The harder it pumps the less efficient it becomes. Sudden death occurs usually because the heart cannot cope with the pressure, so it literally stops. My journey was a lifetime long, not knowing why I was unable to breathe I would feel tired all the time, lack energy, I lost the ability to concentrate. Eventually, my consultant looked at me and said, "Carla, you have exhausted my medical cabinet, I have no other drugs to give you. We have brought your heart rhythm back to normal five times, in a relatively short period of time. Using cardio-version, giving shocks to regulate it, each time we do this the heart muscle is damaged. There is only one possible solution and until we do tests, I cannot confirm it will be possible. That is a transplant." My response, "Are you absolutely sure?"

There followed a series of tests, I spent a week in a London hospital to be prodded and poked, put on treadmills, I gave what felt like gallons of blood. Then I was given the news I would be put on the transplant list.

Back in Sheffield I asked the cardiac surgeon "Are you sure I need this?" His reply was, "We do not give hearts away randomly if you do not have a new heart you will not be here next year. In fact, I cannot promise you will be here in three months. Your heart is kaput!" I stared at him, "Kaput, is that a new medical term? OK, I suppose we better go for it."

After the conversation with the consultant I lay awake in

the hospital bed, my mind started to process what he had said, slowly I realised the implications. I was dying, at forty-two years old. Yes, everyone dies but this was too soon. I would never see my daughter get married, never spend time with my grandchildren, never achieve all those things I dreamt about. As I lay there quietly weeping, John one of the male nurses came over. He asked if I was alright, he made me a cup of tea. He sat with me most of the night, he listened, I talked. He made me smile with his fisherman's tales. I made him smile with my humorous hospital misadventures.

It took six months for a suitable donor to be found, there were two false alarms. I had been issued with a 'Pager.' The hospital would page me when a heart became available, so the pager went wherever I went. Time is important when transplanting organs, once a suitable heart was found, I had four hours to get to the hospital and be ready for the operation.

What I needed to get my head around was, no one had died to give me their heart, they were already dead, or their brain was dead. Part of the preparation for the transplant was time with a psychiatrist, who asked me some odd questions. "Do you realise that any financial state benefits you are receiving now, in respect of your health, will cease when you are well?" I was incredulous, "My health is more important than money!" He smiled, "Good attitude." Then he asked, "Do you believe that people who have an organ transplant can develop characteristics or personality traits from the donor?" I stared at him. "No! That is ridiculous." He laughed, "Actually, a lot of cases in America record patients believe this." I shook my head, "No."

I received a new heart exactly six months after I was added to the list. The operation took place at Sheffield, Northern General Hospital. Someone once said to me "Carla. I think you are so brave to undergo such a serious operation." I replied, "I am not brave, to be brave you have to have a choice, I didn't."

A few hours after the operation I returned to the main ward, I was sitting up in a chair. Within a week I was walking around the ward, by two weeks they said I was well enough to go home. I could not believe the difference it made, I could walk upstairs, bend down and generally move around without fighting for breath. I never looked back.

There were of course, regular biopsies required of the new heart, these were uncomfortable but small price to pay for a new life. The biopsy involved a needle being inserted into my neck, the needle was tiny and had a 'grabber' on the end, a bit like the grabbers you see in slot machines to grasp gifts from a cabinet. This went through my vein, across my chest and down to my heart, then the grabber opened and took some tissue from the heart muscle. The needle made the journey in reverse and the sample tissue was placed in a test tube ready for analysis. This was repeated on three different sections of the heart. The purpose was to monitor and identify, any signs of rejection. The body can reject a transplanted organ at any time. Even years later, medication is used to prevent this happening. After the operation I read that the average life expectancy for the recipient was five years, a few years later this was raised to eleven years. I decided I would look for twenty-five plus.

Five months after my operation I returned to work, with the optimism and vigour of someone who has just cheated death. I wanted to make a difference, to make my new life count.

Now, years later I find I am questioning my motives, what am I trying to prove, why would I risk everything for a job?

Would the people I help even remember me? Stephen, one incident, one bad experience and it feels like I got it all wrong. I am not sure if I can continue.

**The Decision.**

The following morning, I am still uncertain what I want. The only conclusion I came to in a night without sleep, is I am not working alone with Stephen again. A meeting is scheduled for ten in the conference room. Lorrie and Bill will be there, along with Bill's manager, Brian, the head of services. Plus, Alan, Adrian, Shirley, and me. We were the only team members to have worked with Stephen to date.

The meeting is very formal, Debbie has exchanged her role as receptionist, to become minute taker. Lorrie is a good speaker, she somehow manages to make the entire incident about Stephen - his illness, his needs, strategies needed to cope with him, not about staff safety. She manages to make me feel as though I could have stopped the 'incident,' I had somehow allowed it to happen? I listen, feeling more agitated by the minute.

When I am given the opportunity to speak, I am not sure where to start. "Firstly, I know we have a duty of care to the client; the client's needs must be paramount. However, I do also believe that as employers, the Authority has a duty of care to its staff. Staff should not be placed at risk.." Lorrie replies immediately, "You were not at risk, Stephen did not direct his anger towards you, he is more likely to take his anger out on objects." I am angry, I think Bill can sense this, he speaks," I think, as we were not in the house when this happened, we cannot judge who or what Stephen was directing his behaviour at. I hope that this morning we can see a sensible way forward for both Stephen and our staff." Bill looks to me to speak. "I would like to suggest two staff visit Stephen, until we know what we are dealing with." I state my case firmly. Lorrie is getting angry, her face is turning red. "Firstly, we cannot put two staff in, the costs are too high. Secondly, there is nothing for a second person to do and I also feel Stephen may be intimidated with two people there." Lorrie looks to the head of service for confirmation, I have a feeling this has already been discussed before the meeting. I then say, "Well, I refuse to work with Stephen on a one-to-one basis." I can feel the eyes around the room on me. Bill says, "OK. Carla, lets discuss that outside the meeting, if that is your choice." I feel at this point the team and I are being railroaded into agreeing to support Stephen. Lorrie does not let it go, with determination she says, "So Carla, you will let the entire team down, your colleagues, and Stephen. Just because you are not 'happy' working alone with him. I think that is really unprofessional." Tears prick at the back of my eyes, mainly because not one of the team speak up, I know they are all worried, but they are too frightened to speak out. This makes me more resolute.

After the meeting I challenge Shirley, "You said you felt threatened by him why didn't you say something?" Shirley looks down, "He's not that bad. If they put more risk assessments in, we are all aware of his condition now, it should be fine."

During the afternoon I make a point of reading Stephen's file, I need to know my subject if I am challenged. At lunchtime Shirley visits Stephen, if he did do anything controversial, she was not going to say. There is an atmosphere in the office for the first time ever. I feel as though the team are angry because I refuse to work with him. It is not personal against Stephen; it is about safety for everyone. I suppose my promotion is now out of the window. Sometime life throws all the curve-balls at you at once.

**Stephen's file**

The file contains extremely limited information, nothing much that we do not already know. Stephen's mother left when he was ten years old. He was taken out of school at thirteen, tried other schools but failed to settle. One thing I do feel is significant, is the fact he spent two years in a residential mental health facility over in Wolverhampton, they must have detailed notes on him. I try to click on the file, access denied, please submit your mental health registration number, which I do not have. I wonder how I can gain access. I remember Paul is linked to the mental health team maybe he can get me access. I have not spoken with Paul since his revelation about moving to New Zealand. I am still hurt, but I will message him later.

As I contemplate my next move Alan comes into the office, he does not look happy. "Did Sylvia forget your chocolate biscuit?" I smile. "What, sorry what did you say?" Alan looks genuinely upset. "Nothing, what is the matter?" I ask, pointing to the kitchen and making hand gestures for coffee.

In the kitchen Alan says, "I have been at the Police Station with Stephen, he is in a real mess. I am worried he is going to be in a lot of trouble." Alan accepted a coffee. "Why, what on earth has he done?" I am confused, "Has he had an accident?" Alan shakes his head, "No, last evening Stephen believes the coded messages told him he had to go to his neighbours house, to check out their TV screen for additional messages. It was three in the morning. Somehow, Stephen managed to get in, he went straight to their living room, switched on their TV, made himself comfortable on the sofa and sat flicking through the channels looking for messages. The wife heard a noise and came downstairs, to find the front door wide open, she could hear the TV was on. Her husband followed her down, he grabbed in the dark for something to hit the intruder with, in this instance an umbrella. Poor Stephen did not know what hit him.

The neighbour is a big guy, works out regularly, so Stephen had no chance, even if he had considered fighting back. The wife called the police, fortunately because Stephen did not fight back the man just hit him a couple of times then pinned him to the floor and waited for the police to arrive. Stephen has been in custody all night. Lorrie has just taken him home."

Alan looks at me, "He is not a bad lad you know; he is just very ill." I look out of the window, I feel so sorry for Stephen, "I know he is not bad; do you really think that's why I refused to work with him?" Alan shakes his head. "I want him to be safe and our staff to be safe. We do not have enough information about him. I would never want anything like this to happen to him, the poor man he must be frightened and confused?" I leave Alan in the kitchen; I feel quite hurt that he of all people would think of me so negatively. I decide to message Paul.

'Hi, how are you? Do you feel like meeting up this lunchtime? Think we need to clear the air." I hesitate for a few seconds, am I doing this because I want information or because I miss my friend, my lover? Paul replies immediately, 'Hi, sorry in a ridiculously long meeting. Can I meet you after work, supper? My treat. I will pick you up at six thirty. Smiley face.

Everyone is concerned about Stephen; he is the sole subject of conversation for the rest of the afternoon. Of course, there is some sympathy for the neighbour's wife, who was terrified at the time. The police will probably not press charges against the neighbour, Stephen was trespassing. The man had only hit him a couple of times, nevertheless, inflicting him with a bloody nose and a black eye, before he realised there was something odd about Stephen.

Paul calls round at six thirty, we drive to a lovely small pub, set at the edge of the moorlands, it has become our favourite eating place. We make small talk and order drinks and food. 'How was your day?' 'Good weather today.' ;Were you busy today?' Then Paul says, "I am sorry for dropping all that on you the other night. I had been meaning to tell you earlier, just did not know how."

I cannot control my feelings, they come gushing out, "When you say earlier, do you mean before we had the drinks? Of course, I am so difficult to talk to, it is not as though it is a major, life changing decision is it? Oh wait, yes, it is! Of course, I realise that my feelings do not count, after all we hardly know each other." I stop to catch my breath and compose myself. I hate it when my emotions get the better of me. Now I feel like crying. Paul looks wounded. "Well, actually you didn't seem too bothered when I told you, I thought you were pleased for me. You never protested; you just accepted my decision. I thought you didn't care." Paul takes a gulp of his beer.

I am sad that we are disagreeing, we do not have much time now. "OK. can I call a truce? Of course I care, I will miss you like mad. I am fond of you, more than fond. I do not want to spoil

111

the short time we have together." I hold out my hand for a civilised handshake "Friends?" Paul leans over and kisses me, a little too passionately for seven-o-clock in a public bar. We do not speak for a few moments; the waitress arrives with our food and we are both glad for the distraction. Halfway through the main course Paul stops and takes my hand, he is staring into my eyes, "I did not think you would want to come with me." He gently squeezes my hand. "Oh Paul, you know I can't, I have my family here, my children, it's not practical. If only it were nearer, but New Zealand?" Paul laughs a short nervous laugh, "Can I finish please, I knew you would not come, so I had to make a decision. I made the wrong decision. So, I rang them today and withdrew my application. There will be other jobs, maybe not quite so far away." Paul gives me the lopped sided smile I love and winks. It is my turn to reach over and kiss him.

Paul spends the night and I feel ecstatically happy. As we eat breakfast, I tell him about my application to be manager, Paul is incredibly supportive. I then tell him I think I may have blown it with my reaction to Stephen's behaviour. He surprises me by saying he believes I was one hundred percent right. I tell him of my attempts to find out more and being denied access to mental health records. "That's not an issue, we can take a look this evening if you like, I have written lots of risk assessments for mental health, maybe I can help."

**Shirley's Visit**

It is only a couple of days since Stephen's incident with the neighbour, staff report that he has been very subdued and hardly speaks, answering Yes or No questions only. Today Shirley is going. If anyone can make Stephen relax it is Shirley, she has a lovely manner, nothing seems to deter her. She smiles as she leaves the office, "Going to get fish and chips on the way back. Does anyone else want some?" Three of us take Shirley up on her offer and place our orders.

Shirley arrives at Stephen's early, by five minutes, she rings the bell. It takes three more rings before he answers. Opening the door, without speaking he turns and moves quickly into the living room. Shirley follows him in. The TV is on, the screen is flickering, like there is no aerial connected. Stephen is busily drawing, there are several pieces of paper on the settee. "No game today Stephen?" Shirley asks, He shakes his head. "Are you ready for your lunch now?" Again, Stephen shakes his head. He is scribbling so fast, as one page is completed, he starts another. Shirley asks, "Would you mind if I look at your drawings?" Stephen stops, looks at Shirley then slowly passes the small pile of drawings to her. "Wow, Stephen these are really good, you are a very clever artist." She is genuinely impressed with the artwork which appears to be various parts of a spaceship. Stephen stops drawing and goes into the kitchen, Shirley hears him put the kettle on.

Stephen returns, except he does not sit down he starts to move around the room, in a regular pattern around the furniture, he has a glazed expression. Shirley tries to speak but he is no longer listening. He is mumbling. He walks behind her, whispering as though confiding with some unseen person. His pace quickens and he moves quickly, silently around the house. Shirley decides to have a look in the kitchen, maybe find something for his lunch. His coffee cup is by the kettle, with coffee and sugar in, Shirley adds the boiling water.

Without warning, a loud howl echoes around the house, a terrifying sound, half yelling, half screaming. Shirley feels panic. What should she do, no risk assessment?

In the meeting, it was agreed the best method was to stay calm, speak quietly, offer a distraction, a drink, something to eat. Stephen returns to the kitchen, Shirley places his coffee on the worktop and says, "There you are a nice cup of coffee, two sugars. That's right isn't it?" Stephen is still muttering he walks over to the worktop, he lets out another scream, then picks up the steaming hot cup of coffee and launches it at Shirley. The cup hits her directly in the face, she screams, the hot liquid mixes with the blood on her face. Stephen rushes through the living room smashing a few ornaments on the cupboard and wrenching the curtains off their pole. He appears to have superpowers, he pulls the curtain pole off the wall, it hangs down to the floor. He runs out of the front door into the street, yelling obscenities.

Shirley somehow rings the office; I am the only one in. She is struggling to explain, I can hear the fear in her voice, she is injured. As I leave, I ask reception to get hold of Bill and tell him I have gone to Stephen's house, that he is having another incident. As I arrive, Shirley is at the door, her tee shirt is covered in blood, she has been crying. She is holding a tea towel to her face; it is now covered in blood. "I am sorry, he ran off in the direction of the park." I usher Shirley inside; I want to see how badly she is hurt. There is a broken cup on the floor. Shirley gently moves the towel from her face and jokingly says, "He is a good shot." I see She took a direct hit on the bridge of her noses, there is a gash just below her left eye, it is still bleeding. Her face is bright red from the boiling coffee. Shirley gives a slight shiver; I wonder if she is in shock. "Come on, we are going to Accident and Emergency, I want that cut checked." I'm really concerned, it looks dreadful, but am trying not to panic. We lock the house as we leave. Fortunately, we are only five minutes from the local hospital. I take Shirley in and the nurse escorts her straight through to the treatment area. I ring Bill, he is at the house. Lorrie is apparently on annual leave. I explain about Shirley's injury. I then suggest we get in touch with his brother Harold, as Stephen was last seen heading towards the park. "Already done that, he is on his way." Bill sounds odd, "Listen Carla, I am sorry I did not back you on this, you are right we need more information, more strategies. This young man is a liability." I am grateful for Bill's recognition, "I think I may have something by tomorrow, some useful information, maybe we can meet in the morning?" Bill agrees, then says he must go  Stephen's brother has arrived, with Stephen.

The staff at the hospital treat Shirley's cut, they glue the skin together. This they advise is quicker and less likely to cause scaring. They say she is fortunate that most of the blood came from her nose, which thankfully is not broken. Her nose will be tender for a few days and the glued stitches will come off in about five days. Shirley has minor scalding to her cheek and neck; staff add a cold compress and provide antibiotic cream. They give her painkillers, advise regular cold compresses to her face and neck, and suggest she goes home to rest.

I take Shirley home and stay until I feel sure she is calm and relaxed. She has been fortunate, there should not be any scars. The only scars are internal, psychological. Shirley has definitely lost her sparkle. Bill rings to say Stephen is fine, his brother is staying for the evening. He thanks Shirley and myself for acting quickly, I suspect he is embarrassed by the events of the day.

**Strategies**

After supper Paul and I look at the file from Brownley

Residential Centre regarding Stephen. It seems he did not have the best of times there. For the first three months he had to be restrained on his bed several times by staff, using soft nylon restraint bracelets, attached to his arms and legs. He had one serious episode, when he smashed up furniture and terrorised other patients in the dining hall. During this period Stephen was first given anti-psychotic medication to control his symptoms. One doctor appeared to take a particular interest in Stephen, a Doctor Ahmed, he studied and recorded Stephen's patterns of behaviour and put into place a five-point strategy. He looked first for possible triggers and then at strategies to avoid them. Having worked with Stephen these made sense.

He noted that criticism of any degree, however slight, could trigger Stephen to shout, rant, and curse. This could continue for several hours. He discovered placing Stephen alone, either by withdrawing staff or placing him in a quiet area, helped him to calm down more quickly.

Interruptions were a second possible trigger, if he had cleared a table and someone placed dirty dishes on it, if he was listening to music and the dinner gong rang, or if he were in the middle of his game. This could result in screaming and throwing objects. Dr Ahmed found that by agreeing a timetable first and staff following it, Stephen maintained a degree of control. If he did not feel well, his process for dealing with it was anger, if in pain, he became angry, often retreating into a shell and refusing to communicate. Staff were made aware, so that Stephen's physical health needs were monitored. Sudden loud noises sounds on TV or from outside, could cause Stephen to shout and scream obscenities. Dr Ahmed suggested meditation and music therapy.

Finally, it was noted that he did not like to be controlled, to be given orders - 'tidy your room, make your lunch'. Often, he would deal with this trigger, by pacing over and over, around objects and screaming. A planned exercise routine was proposed to use excess energy and help Stephen deal with negative emotions. I had my basis for new Risk Assessments and a structure for a planned programme of support. Paul and I worked together to write six basic Risk Assessments.

I spoke to Bill the next morning, I presented the draft risk assessments. Bill suggested I put them to Lorrie. This did not come easily to me; I had done the work. However, I followed Bill's guidance because in the long term and the bigger scheme of things, we needed to function as a team.

By the end of the week Lorrie and I had put together a planned programme of support, with all the appropriate paperwork. Lorrie, I found was extremely good at interpreting the strategies and we worked well together.

Stephen continues to have support, he joined a meditation group, a music therapy group, also an art group. He spends less time on his games and has become more interactive with staff, going shopping, and out walking each week. His medication was reintroduced by the medical team and his symptoms are reduced. Stephen has progressed with his artistic skills and his home is now full of his pictures.

Staff have built up good working relationships with him and encourage him to discuss any issues or concerns, as much as possible. It is not the best solution for Stephen, he is still isolated at home for a large percentage of the day. There are still days when Stephen's behaviour places himself and others at risk. Both Stephen and the staff are continually learning new strategies, to help adjust and manage his behaviour, so he can continue to live independently. Sometimes, despite our best efforts we fail to meet all our clients' needs, which is frustrating for everyone concerned.

# Chapter Four

# Chantelle

'All the roads you regret for not going to the end, represent the alternative lives you may have lived.'

Mehmet Murat Idan

### First Visit

We stand on a narrow, cold, concrete stairwell, I am with Chris, a social worker, seconded from the mental health team. He has invited me along to meet his client who will be supported by our team, the client has a history of sexual flirting, so I assume, as a female, I am there for his protection. Chris is overly cautious, not a risk taker, a stickler for the rules. This probably explains why he is one of the few social workers who wears a tie every day and carries a briefcase. I am thankful he has left the briefcase in the car; it is not a place where anyone who might be associated with authority is welcome.

"Does this staircase just lead to her flat?" The reason I ask is twofold, it appears to have no lighting and each stair is full of discarded cigarette ends. Chris nods and looks down, "Oh, the cigarette ends? They are from her customers; they wait on the stairs for their turn." I look at him doubting what he said,

"You mean she is a prostitute?" Chris gives me a half smile,

"Sort of, she sells favours to finance her drug habit." Chris knocks on the door, a few seconds later it is opened by Chantelle. She is beautiful. She has the look of a top model, long legs, lovely figure and blonde hair that falls in soft curls. She is wearing an expensive negligee set, in pink silk. Prostitution must pay well, I think. She invites us in, her voice is soft and has a childlike quality, I have read on the brief she is twenty-two years old, single and lives alone.

Chris leads the conversation, asking her how she has been, if she managed to keep the doctor's appointment, he had arranged for her. She had not. I look around, the small flat is decorated with style, not my style, a glamorous look. The sofa and armchair are of a soft white leather, with a dozen or more pink and gold brocade cushions, scattered randomly. There is a large white fur rug in front of the gas fire. An elaborate, gold coloured mirror hangs over the fireplace. White curtains are draped at the large window, which overlooks a garden area with trees. I could easily believe I am sitting in some luxury apartment in Kensington, had I not just driven through a dismal council estate and entered up the concrete staircase.

Chris asks Chantelle if she is eating, she replies, "Of course, I went out last evening to the new restaurant in town, the Turkish one, it was lovely. Have you tried it yet?" Both Chris and I shake our heads, I have seen the ads for the place, it is pretty classy, average main course around twenty-five pounds, which is out of my budget range. Chris explains why I am there, the abbreviated version, "Carla is one of the team who will be working with you, to help you with your budgeting so you do not get into difficulties again." Chris then directs his explanation to me, "Chantelle got into a mess with her money, did not pay her bills and lost her benefits because she failed to meet appointments. She borrowed some money from some pretty nasty loan sharks, they came after her, took her TV set, her stereo, what else did they take Chantelle?" I could see her thinking for a moment,

"They took my I-phone, my Gucci sunglasses, my Cartier Ballon Bleu watch. Oh, and my ghd platinum hair straighteners." Chantelle sighed resolutely. I am secretly thinking, my oh my what hardship, poor little rich girl! Despite this flouting of money, there is something vulnerable, likeable about Chantelle.

I ask her, "What sort of things would you like support with?" She concentrates for a while then says, "I would like to get a proper job, so I can move away from this area. I do not have any qualifications, my education was, well it was disrupted. So maybe I could look at going to college. I always wanted to study law, but I suppose I left it too late for that. Maybe I'm not clever enough?" I feel confident this is something we can support her with, "I think it's a perfect age to study, you know what you want to achieve, nothing is beyond your reach if you are willing to work for it. We can go to the college and see what is available next week if you like?"

"Really! That would be great, will you come in with me, I am a little nervous?" she asks, Chantelle looks genuinely interested, if this young woman wants to turn her life around then I am sure we can help her. "Of course, how about I pick you up here at ten on Monday morning?" We confirm, I will also support Chantelle with shopping and budgeting. As we leave, she thanks us both for our time.

When we reach the cars I say to Chris, "She is a really nice person, I wonder what happened to her?" Chris smiles, "I will send you her file access. She is clear at the moment; I have been trying to get her off the coke. When I first met her, she was virtually anorexic, she was not eating, I think mainly because she could not afford food and cocaine. I am hoping we have turned a corner now." Chris opens his extremely clean, polished ford, which smells of vanilla. I climb into my car. 'Must clean my car,' I think, noting the empty water bottles and papers on the rear seat. "I will be in touch." Chris says as he drives away.

I have another appointment at two o' clock, there is just enough time to grab a sandwich and write up my notes. The office is unusually quiet, "Where is everyone?" I ask Adrian, not expecting an answer, he looks up from his computer, "Don't know, suppose it's a bit early for lunch." I glance at my emails, Chris has already sent me the link for Chantelle's file, I will look at it tomorrow, Saturday is a quieter day in the office, most of the calls are early morning. I eat my usual tuna and sweetcorn on brown, I think I am becoming boring. Maybe I should suggest to Paul we try out the new Turkish place, to hell with the costs. I finish my lunch leave for my next call.

It takes me a while to find the house. It is a nice estate full of individually designed bungalows and detached houses, set around small cul de sacs. This confuses the lady trapped inside my Satellite Navigation, and she keeps insisting I take the next right to correct my error, only next right is another cul de sac. Eventually I find the dormer bungalow, it is a semi, the neighbour is out in the garden and nods as I arrive. I am here to see Dorothy Green; she should have arrived home from hospital about an hour ago. Dorothy has just had a replacement hip; she already has two knee replacements. I ring the bell. No reply. I ring it again and tap on the door. Still no reply.

The neighbour has been watching, she calls over, "If you are here to see Dorothy, she is definitely in, I saw the ambulance bring her at one o'clock." I say "Thank you" then try. No reply. The lady from next door is now standing next to me, "She is definitely in there, her hearing is not too good." I wander over to the living room window, "She is on the floor!" The neighbour looks horrified, "I have a key" she shouts, as she dashes back over the drive. Two minutes later we are in. Dorothy is conscious, she smiles when I bend over, "Try not to move Dorothy, where does it hurt?" Dorothy says "Everywhere, it hurts everywhere, I was just trying to get upstairs to the toilet, lost my footing, damn well hurts." I unlock my phone, "Dorothy I am going to ring an ambulance." As I am speaking to the operator, I see the neighbour hooking her arm under Dorothy's arm, "Do not move her." I shout, probably a little too forcefully. The neighbour lets go. Five minutes later the ambulance arrives, the young driver walks in and says, "Dorothy, we cannot leave you alone for a minute, what have you been up too?" It seems it is the same ambulance that brought her home. The two men manage to get Dorothy onto a stretcher, "we are taking her in to get her checked over, chances are she will probably be kept in." The driver informs me. Once Dorothy is in the ambulance the other guy comes back for her medication, which I discover in the kitchen. "She was sent home without any equipment in place, her toilet is upstairs that is why she fell," I explain, "Don't worry, this happens a lot, people are sent home too soon, because they are short of beds. It's crazy because we just end up taking them back in." He shrugs his shoulders and leaves. We lock the house and leave, the neighbour retaining the key. "For next time." She says, I am not sure if she is serious.

The office is busier on my return, Adrian comments, "You were quick?" "Yes", I reply, I cannot be bothered explaining, I write the incident on Dorothy's file. Everyone is buzzing about the Christmas Party, it is not the official one, this is a private function which has been organised by a local DJ, who Bill knows. It is a nineteen sixties evening, those of us who are going have

123

agreed to dress up for the occasion, even the men are getting involved. Mike is coming as David Bowie and Lucas is going to be Jimi Hendrix. Shirley and I are still debating who we can be, She is thinking of Sandy Shaw, but cautious about not wearing shoes. It is a week tomorrow, so we do not have long to prepare.

That evening there is a premiership match on TV which Paul wants to watch. I am feeling weary, so decide to have a long relaxing shower. We have a take-away curry. Whilst Paul is glued to the set, with just the odd grunt of "No!" I decide to check my emails. My daughter has sent me pictures of the hotel they have booked for their next holiday, it looks lovely, I write back and give her what little news I have. I am daydreaming about the meeting with Chantelle, why not go back to college, she is only twenty-two.

I was twenty-three when I returned to education. I left school at fifteen with a school Bible, as my only proof of attendance. Although, in the last two years there had been little attendance. School and I agreed to disagree, they could not teach me, I would not or could not learn. At twenty-three years I moved to London, I wanted to get a job in human resources. I very quickly realised that without qualifications there was no way. I went and spoke to a lady at the local college and she would prove to have a great influence on my life. She was from Liverpool, she commented on my Northern accent. I admitted that my accent was already having a negative effect on my life.

"I know it sounds silly, but people in the South, just assume I am thick, because of the way I speak." Miss Moore laughed, "I do not think you are silly; I had a really broad Liverpool accent when I first went to University. People there automatically assumed I was not as bright as others; it was like I had to work harder to prove myself." I was really impressed with her story. Miss Moore guided me through my first year. We agreed I should study O-Levels first, in English language, Literature, Mathematics, Government & Politics and Sociology. I would study A-level in Sociology and Psychology in my second year. I only agreed to the Government & Politics because Miss Moore taught this. She also taught Sociology and Psychology.

My first day at college was daunting, the site was so big. I was a little late for my first class, English Language. I sat at the back and listened. I thought to myself, this is going to be easy, use a capital letter to start a sentence, commas, full stops. Really basic stuff, no problem. At the end of class I had very few notes. The tutor thanked everyone for coming to the 'English as a Second Language Class'. I was in the wrong class and wrong building. I never told a soul.

Sociology, apart from the use of a strange vocabulary which I had never heard before, was pretty straightforward. Then the tutor said she expected a six-hundred-word essay about 'Family life in Great Britain'. I waited till the end of class then approached her, I asked, "What is an essay?" Simple question, for someone who missed out on their education. She explained, I grasped it was another word for story. Easy. Thirty-six hours, I wrote and re-wrote my essay, I cried, I tore up pages. I debated the logic of it with my other half. It would be two weeks before I got my work back. I could not see it for the red ink. Spelling mistakes, grammar errors, unconfirmed quotes, personal opinions the list was endless. At the bottom of the page was written in capital letters. THIS READS LIKE A FAIRY STORY, QUOTE ALL SOURCES. BUY A DICTIONARY.

I took this advice. So, it was I muddled through my first year, I ran a home, worked part-time in a supermarket, yet managed to somehow achieve five O levels all with good grades,

Sociology at A grade. The following year I achieved two A Levels at grade B. I then obtained a place at Brunel University. Regretfully, I did not take this up, for financial and domestic reasons. Instead I did a certificate in HR management (personnel as it was then called) at Acton Technical College, on day release from my first job as a personnel officer.

This is why I have every confidence that Chantelle can do this if she puts her mind to it.

## Second Visit

It is Monday morning, though it is just another day to me. When you work shifts over seven days, your days off vary, I love this aspect of the work, I can shop on a Tuesday when everywhere is quiet, I can do my housework in peace, there are rarely interruptions during the week. Few salespeople ring up and roads are generally quieter. I am going to collect Chantelle at nine-forty-five to go to the college, I made an appointment for us to speak with one of the guidance workers, so Chantelle can find out exactly what she needs.

I read most of her file over the weekend, it is not reading for the faint-hearted. Her mother left just after she was born, it is believed she went back to America. She was raised by her father. There is no record of other family, no aunts, uncles, or grandparents. At the age of ten Chantelle told a teacher that she had been inappropriately 'touched' by her father, this was investigated, she was placed in foster care, her father served a prison sentence. She struggled in foster care, unable to settle; her behaviour became challenging and she was moved to four different placements. At secondary school, she was a popular student and did well in most subjects, excelling in English language. Eventually she remained with the same foster carers for four years. When she was fourteen, she claimed the eldest son of the foster carers had raped her. He lived with his wife and two young children. Chantelle had been their regular babysitter. She later said the son had started by 'touching her inappropriately' when she was thirteen. The police were involved charges were made and Chantelle was moved to another foster home.

She was involved in a further incident when she was fifteen, she was abducted by a group of five males between the ages of sixteen and twenty. The abduction took place in a busy area of town, no witnesses came forward. She was discovered half naked, with scratches and bruises, in a field the next day, by a local farmer. The police investigated and found evidence she had been raped. There was also evidence that she had taken or been given against her will, cocaine .

Shortly afterwards she was admitted to hospital having taken a mixture of painkillers, sleeping pills and alcohol. She was placed in residential care, with support from the mental health team. She made two further attempts to take her life in the following year. Chantelle was suffering from depression, caused by the emotional and psychological effects of the sexual attacks. Counselling sessions were arranged. She began to self-harm, she inflicted deep cuts at the top of her thighs and was referred to a specialist mental health unit. During this time, she began to dramatically lose weight, she also suffered from panic attacks. She continued to have suicidal thoughts for several months and remained in the special unit for two years. At the age of eighteen, she demonstrated more stability and had developed ways to cope with the emotional turmoil. She continued with the counselling and was eventually helped back into society.

Chantelle was first homed in an adult placement, with

an older couple. she stayed there for three weeks. The mental health team and police discovered her sleeping rough in the railway station. Eventually she was given a one bedroom flat. Support was provided daily, though she frequently refused to engage with staff. Her progress was monitored by people from the mental health team, she received financial support in the form of state benefits. Support was required to help her manage her budget. She would spend the week's money on clothing, leaving herself with nothing to eat. Then her life appeared to improve, she began to look after herself, joined a gym and dressed well. She said her special friend was helping her.

Last year Chantelle was referred to the drug and alcohol unit. She had been found wandering in town, confused. Blood tests revealed a mixture of alcohol and cocaine. It is believed she is involved in prostitution to supplement her cocaine addiction.

Chantelle is waiting when I arrive, she looks incredibly smart and chic, with a navy-blue suit, white blouse and navy-blue stiletto-heeled shoes. Her hair is scooped up into a loose bun. She is wearing make-up; but it is not obvious. I feel quite dowdy at the side of her, she is tall and slim and carries an air of confidence. "Hi, wow! You look smart. Love the outfit." I smile. Chantelle blushes, "You don't think it is too much do you? I was not sure what to wear." "Not at all. It is important to feel good about yourself at any meeting." I secretly wish I had made more of an effort. I drive us to the college.

The lady I have arranged to see is Mrs Graith, we report to reception. Mrs Graith is a middle-aged lady, slightly over-weight and she walks with a wobble. She smiles and asks, "Is it Chantelle?" She obviously thinks I am the client, I point to Chantelle, "This is Chantelle, I am Carla, we spoke on the phone." She smiles, shakes both our hands, and leads us into a small side room, where there is a table and four chairs."Now, how can I help you Chantelle?" I look at Chantelle, just for a second, I think she is not going to answer, then she says. "I would like to go back to college to study law, is that possible?" Mrs Graith beams, "Why we have several options available, what qualifications do you have?" Chantelle looks flustered, "None, that is why I am here. I want to learn." Mrs Graith looks stern then she softens, "OK, what subjects did you like at school?" Chantelle tells Mrs Graith she likes English, language and Literature, History and Geography. There follows a detailed conversation about the best study options for her, full or part-time - subjects which are relevant to her chosen career. Chantelle becomes deeply involved in the discussion, she asks questions and appears keen to make the right decisions. Mrs Graith produces a number of leaflets about the courses, the structure of classes and details of the college opportunities.

After an hour we leave, Chantelle is clutching an armful of brochures. In the Reception area she smiles and asks, "Could you hold these a moment please, I just need the toilet?" she passes me the information and I take a seat. Five minutes later she appears. Something is different.

She looks at me, "Listen, I have just had a call, my friend wants to meet me for lunch, then we are going into town to have some beauty treatment, facial and eyebrows. Can you take the papers, I will get them from you when I next see you? Got to go, I think there is a train in ten minutes." With that she turns and starts walking towards the door, "Wait, Chantelle. I will walk back with you as far as the car park." she strides on, I am now walking several paces behind her.

The street is busy, lots of cars and shoppers. Then I hear a horn beeping, a man is hanging out of his taxi window, "Hi,

Chantelle you free later?" He is laughing mockingly. Another beep, another taxi, "Chantelle, Chantelle do you have time for me?" The taxi drives on. Chantelle has not slowed down and appears to have ignored the shouting. Another taxi passes, this one just gives a prolonged beep. As we reach the car park I stop, Chantelle is oblivious of my presence, her behaviour is hyper, she has definitely taken something. I open the car door, to hear another car beeping loudly, this time there are two men in a taxi, they are more explicit in what they want Chantelle to do. Chantelle disappears into the railway station.

I sit in my car for a few moments, I feel angry, frustrated, I feel as though the entire morning has been a waste of time. I am now going back to work, "Chantelle" is spending time at the beauticians, eating lunch with her friend. I have to think about money, how much I can spend, what I can afford. Then I chastise myself, her file says she is unable to control her spending. Chantelle lives in the moment. The drivers, I found unnerving, were they clients of hers? They all knew her name. What shame would her mother feel? Would she even care?

Cocaine, which is what I believe Chantelle took in the toilets, causes the person to feel energetic, mentally alert, talkative. Maybe there is no friend, no lunch, or beautician? If she has snorted the cocaine, she will probably be on a high for thirty minutes or so, her behaviour was erratic. I never looked at her eyes, maybe I should have checked them, her pupils will have been dilated. I wonder where she might have gone. Is she safe? Should I have stopped her? How? I feel as though she has deliberately made a fool of me, yet here I am worrying about her. I drive back to the office.

Paul messages to say he will not be coming round this evening; he is going for a game of pool with his mates. I feel quite relieved, I want some time alone. Lacey is in the kitchen, she appears with a large plate of Chinese food, noodles, chicken, and rice. It smells delicious, she is tucking into the mass as she walks back to her seat. I smile at her "Gosh Lacey that smells good!" Lacey swallows and nods towards the kitchen, "There is a lot more in there, if you want some help yourself." This time I decide to accept Lacey's offer and obtain myself a plate full of food. Comfort eating, the best remedy.

### Third Visit

I have tried for over a week to contact Chantelle her phone is switched off. On the three visits I made to her flat there was no reply, I spoke with Chris, he did not appear concerned, apparently this is the way Chantelle engages with support, randomly at best. It is difficult to see how I might help someone who chooses when she will co-operate, whose life is so chaotic, no one seems to know or care where she is.

I press the doorbell again, there is a buzzer entry system, if she is in, she can open the door by pressing a button. After the third ring I decide I am wasting my time and turn to leave, I then hear the door click open. The stairs are dark, a few empty lager cans have now joined the cigarette butts. Inside the flat I can hear Chantelle in the kitchen. She comes in wearing a casual jogging suit and slippers. She looks different, tired, thinner? Her hair is tied back in a ponytail, she has no make-up and her skin has a faint yellow tinge. "Hi, I did not realise it was you, do you want a cup of tea or coffee? I have just made myself one." I nod, "Thank you, I was just about to give up, I thought you were out." I look at her, she is distant, her eyes are heavy, lack of sleep maybe. Chantelle returns with two cups. She smiles. "Sorry only had coffee." I take the cup, "That's fine. I have been trying to get hold of you all week, I was worried about you." Chantelle has a puzzled expression. "Why?" It occurs to me that she has probably never had anyone worry about her, I suppose the foster carers did, but she had been much younger. "Where were you? I tried to call but your phone was off."

She is now staring at a pile of boxes, suitcases, odd shoes, a hoover, ironing board all stacked in one corner of the room, I had not noticed them. "Are you having a clear out?" I ask. She shakes her head, "no, I think I have rats. I can hear them at night scratching in the cupboard, they make funny sounds, like they are talking to each other," She grins. "Rat language! No, but seriously I hate rats, they are destructive, they attack humans you know. They have sharp claws and teeth. I have always been afraid of them since I was a child."

I stand. "Mind if I take a look?" I peer into the cupboard there is nothing, no signs of rat faeces or of chewing. "Have you actually seen a rat?" I ask. "No but I know they are there, I have seen their eyes, in the night they come out, they stare at me," she physically shivers. "Would you like me to have the pest control officer take a look, he can put down some poison?" We agree this will be a good idea. I explain, "when I make the appointment, I will call you, it is important that you are home to let him in. Is your phone working OK? I could not reach you on it" Chantelle shakes her head, "I ran out of credit last week but its working now."

We talk about our visit to the college; Chantelle appears to have completely forgotten her strange behaviour and asks me if I have the leaflets. We look at them and the information sheet Mrs Graith collated. We talk about options and time frames, she is extremely bright, her memory for details is particularly good.

My curiosity is aroused."Tell me, why are you so frightened of rats?" She looks at me, as if considering a complex puzzle.

"I think I was four years old, that is my first memory. I had done something naughty; I think I put wax crayon on the wall. My father was really angry. He put me in the cellar. We lived in an old terraced house; the coal cellar was only small, just big enough for a few sacks of coal to be stored. There was a little light from the wooden hatch, where the coal man would tip his sacks. I remember being scared in case he made a delivery and did not see me, I thought I would be buried and die under a pile of coal. So, I sat on the bottom step and waited. It was then that I first heard them, scurrying along the floor, I could not see them clearly, I was not sure what they were. I could just see eyes; I raised my legs off the floor and made myself into a tight ball, so they could not see me. I was terrified. I have no idea how long I was down there.

When I was taken out, I tried extremely hard to be good, I must have been very naughty because I made several visits to the cellar. On one occasion, two rats sat watching me, I tried to talk to them. I thought maybe we could be friends, I reached out to stroke it and it bit my finger. I screamed and screamed so loud that my Father came and dragged me out. My finger was sore for a long time. The good thing was father stopped putting me in the cellar for a little while.

Then one evening, when I came home from school, I switched the oven on, as I had been instructed to do, so supper would be ready when he got in from work. I forgot about it and went upstairs to do my homework." I interrupt, "Sorry Chantelle, how old were you then?" "I was nearly ten. Supper was burned and father was so angry, he put me in the cellar, this time he wrapped a scarf around my mouth so I could not scream. I spent the entire night in the cellar, I felt as though I could not breathe, I tried to remove the scarf it was too tight. I soiled myself, father had to bath me the next morning. He said he was sorry, that I was his little princess, he bathed me and wrapped me in a big fluffy towel. I stayed home from school for the rest of the week. Of course, that was when things really started to get bad."

I could see by her face that this story had stirred up lots of deeply held emotions. I am not a psychologist, I am uncertain what to do with this information. I give Chantelle a hug. "That was awful for you, I am glad you felt able to talk to me about it. I am so glad you are safe now." I watch the emotion on her face, sadness, and fear, yet somewhere in her, there is also a determination to survive.

"I will arrange for the council to come tomorrow to check the flat. Do you feel alright to be here tonight? Have you got a friend, someone who could stay with you?" She shakes her head, "No I will be fine, I have to go out later to meet a friend so maybe they will stay."

I decide to ask about the taxi drivers, "Did you hear the taxi drivers calling you when we left the college?" She shakes her head. "Oh, I just wondered how they all know you?" She gives a half smile, "I use taxis a lot."

Before I leave, we discuss practical matters, Chantelle tells me she still has ten pounds left and will receive her benefits the following morning. She confirms that her diet has suffered recently because she did not shop for food. We agree to go together to the supermarket tomorrow. Chantelle takes a note of my work and mobile numbers. I ask her to read the college information then if she still wants to go ahead, we can go to the enrolment day. I advise her to leave all the things out of the cupboard until the man has been to lay the poison. I suspect it may only be a mouse, whatever it is, it will be removed. I do not ask her about the friend she is meeting; I do not want to pry too much. If I appear too inquisitive, she may back away completely, it is about building mutual trust and respect. I say goodbye and we agree for me to come the following day at ten-thirty.

      I glance at my watch, damn it almost twelve, I have to meet Tony the social worker, across the other side of town in half an hour, it is going to be a late lunch today. I drive around the town using the bypass, it is slightly further but quicker. I stop at a mini market and purchase a small bottle of lemonade; I need the sugar more than the liquid. The address is in the middle of the Heald Estate, an area I am not happy about working in but at least it is daylight. I arrive at the same time as Tony. We are meeting the client for the first time, the referral has come from a concerned family member, his brother. The client, Liam Shawcross is forty years old, ex-military, he is having treatment for anxiety and depression. His elder brother is worried that Liam may harm himself. He is also concerned that Liam is displaying unusual behaviour, dressing inappropriately, and refusing to leave the house. Liam also has a number of pets.

  We walk together to the house. A standard two bedroomed semi, it was originally the family home. Liam's wife left about six months after he returned from active duty. Tony knocks, the door is opened almost immediately, we both step back. Liam is standing in the doorway. He is dressed in full combat gear, including boots and a head-wrap, he is tall, well built, and looks angry and aggressive. Tony introduces us and explains that Liam's brother had asked us to call, he thought that we may be able to help Liam. He stands back, "Enter." I am already feeling uncomfortable. "Please take a seat, I have told John I am fine, there really is nothing to worry about. I am afraid he has wasted your time." He sits down on the armchair.

"Do you mind if we just have a little chat while we are here, it will not take long." Tony asks. "OK. What do you want to know?"

"We understand that you served in the military, when was your last tour of duty?" Liam sits upright, "Why?" Tony shifts in his seat. "We are just trying to get a picture as to why John is so worried." Liam is considering Tony's explanation. I look around, there are several plastic and glass containers and tanks around the room. To my horror I see they contain spiders. A large Black Widow is staring at me. There are lizards in other tanks then my worst nightmare - four tanks containing snakes. I would really like to leave now.

"OK. I concluded my service two years ago after serving in Iraq and Afghanistan." What Liam is not telling us is he was medically discharged, following an inquiry into 'inappropriate use of force'. He and two other officers had entered a building, where snipers had been seen. They had shot two snipers, then burst the door on another room and two unarmed women were shot. Liam had not actually fired a shot, but the two women died at the scene.

"So, how has it been, you were in the forces a long time I understand. How have you found adapting to civilian life?" Liam leans down the side of his chair, he lift up a large snake, a Boa Constrictor. I stand. I have never liked snakes and one this size is definitely terrifying. Liam watches me then turns and places the Boa in a large terrarium along the back wall. "That's Nell, I forgot she was out for her morning stretch, she is perfectly harmless." I am still standing contemplating a quick exit. "There is nothing else out for a walk is there?" I ask nervously. Liam laughs," no you are probably safer in here than out there in the streets." My eyes are drawn to another case, I can see two scorpions. I look at

Tony, he appears relaxed and asks, "How old is Nell?" Liam is happy to talk about her, "she is only three years old, still a baby, she will grow much bigger. Nell is really gentle. Would you like to hold her?" Tony declines. Liam walks around the room, describing his menagerie of insect and reptiles, I wonder if it is legal to have so many species in one place? Tony is fascinated, he asks lots of questions and Liam is only too pleased to describe and instruct his new disciple, my skin is crawling. Liam looks at me, "You not happy about my little friends?" I answer honestly, "No, I can never see the point of having a pet without four legs and fur." I try not to look too intimidated.

Liam is now describing the strength of poison each creature has and its ability to defend itself. I am no longer listening, I am looking around the room, under the glass case containing Nell, are two boxes, the first has a label stating dried food. The other is open, I stare, it contains knives and hand grenades. Propped against the wall is a rifle with full bayonet attached. Hanging on the wall are two Japanese swords and two machetes. I am really feeling uncomfortable.

I look at my watch, "Tony, sorry to interrupt this very interesting conversation, but I have another appointment at two and I need to leave." Tony looks across and nods. "Sorry Liam, duty calls, maybe I could come back again to learn more about your very interesting pets?" Liam stands up, "I do not think so, your work here is done." I wonder at this point if he is going to kill us both and feed me to Nell. Tony replies, "OK, Liam, you seem to have got things sorted, I will put in my notes no help required, is that alright." Liam smirked "That is just fine with me." By now I have the front door open, I am convinced he will not kill us in the street. As we leave Liam closes the door behind us.

"Let's drive around the corner and chat," Tony suggests as we reach the cars. I park up in a lay-by, Tony pulls in behind me. "Fucking Hell excuse my French, that man is a walking time bomb, it looks like he is about to declare war on the world. I am definitely not sure how stable he is." Tony is more disturbed than I am, "at one point I thought we would only be leaving there in a box!" I laugh. "What are we going to do, we cannot send staff in there?" Tony looks serious." No. This is way out of our depth, I am going to the Police Station to make a full report. They may want to interview you too and take a written statement. Are you free now?"

We attend the station and make full reports. A few days later we hear that armed police have arrested Liam for possession of illegal weapons, propaganda related to terrorism, plus an assortment of illegally imported dangerous species. We have no further contact, though rumours suggest Liam has been taken to a secure mental health establishment for treatment.

**Fourth Visit**

I have not contacted Paul, maybe I am being stubborn? I have been alone too long. I get up, another cold grey day, I wonder what it would be like to wake up to blue skies and sunshine. Yesterday I arranged for the 'Exterminator' to visit Chantelle's flat at eleven today, I tried calling her several times during the afternoon but there was no reply. I will ring her again when I get to the office. Mr Tom is still asleep, I marvel at the life of a cat - sleep, eat, exercise and play.

I ring Chantelle, the message is the same, 'this number is not available at the moment, please try later.' I write up my report on the 'Liam' visit. These days no one knows who lives next door, when I was a child, we knew all our neighbours. Although we did not live in each other's houses, we knew the families, their names, where they worked, their children. I expect Liam's neighbours would not be happy, knowing they lived just a few feet away from so many deadly creatures and weapons. I try Chantelle's number again.

"Hello." Chantelle answers in a sleepy voice. "Good morning Chantelle, it's Carla, just ringing to let you know the man is coming at eleven to put some poison down. I will be there at ten thirty." I wait for a response. "OK." The line goes dead. 'Thank you, Carla, how helpful of you, I look forward to seeing you,' I say to myself; I never understand the complete lack of manners in some people.

When I arrive, Chantelle is showered and dressed, she has already added make-up and looks fresh, in a neat green pinafore with a cream jumper. We have coffee, "Did you have a nice time yesterday?" I ask. She looks unsure, "err, yes we did." It feels as though she does not want to discuss yesterday. "Do you have plans today?" I am hoping for a positive response. "No, well no plans, I may be working later." She replies. We sit quietly for a few moments; I am relieved when the buzzer goes. The man is in his fifties, dressed in a full white overall, complete with hood. He is wearing disposable gloves, perched on his head is a full facial visa. A little over the top for what I feel is probably a lone mouse. He looks in the cupboard, checks around the flat, he looks confused. "There are no signs of infestation, no trails. You reported the vermin had been seen in the cupboard, I will leave a couple of traps in there. You don't have other pets, do you?" Chantelle shakes her head. "OK." He places the traps in the cupboard, tells her to check them tomorrow and leaves. "Well that was quick," I stand and start to move some of the things back in the cupboard, "Probably best not to put everything back, or you will have to take it out again tomorrow."

As I lift one of the boxes a photo falls to the floor, it is a young woman, at first, I think it is Chantelle, the dress style is from the seventies. "That is my mother, just before she left." Chantelle takes the photo from me. "You look a lot like her." I suggest. "Yes, people say that. We are two different people though, I would never leave my child, if I ever have one." I can understand Chantelle's anger. "Do you know why she left?" I am not expecting a positive answer. "My father said she liked men; she was sleeping around. Then one day he woke to find her gone." Chantelle pushes the photograph back into the box.

We both return to our seats. "Do you know what I do for a living?" she asks. I am unsure how to answer, "I think you do whatever is necessary to survive. I do think you have a lot of potential to build a career. You have style and taste, looking at your flat and the way you dress. You are bright and very pretty." Chantelle is considering my comments, "I am a prostitute, I sell my body for sex. I need money to buy cocaine." This is said almost as a challenge, "I know." I say and smile. "That is OK. We all have to do what we can. How long have you been using cocaine?" Chantelle looks younger somehow, she is calculating, "maybe a year, or a little longer. I hate it you know. I used to think people who take drugs are stupid. Now I feel as though I cannot do anything without it. When I don't take it, I have no energy, no motivation. I do not inject it; I am scared of needles! How daft is that." Chantelle laughs.

"I can understand that, I have been scared of needles all my life, since I fought the nurse who tried to give me a measles vaccine." I smile.

"I usually sniff it or rub it on my gums. I know it can do serious damage to the body, yet I still need it. I get lots of headaches and nose bleeds, I have heard of people having seizures, that scares me but when I am high it does not matter. I cannot sleep and I am never hungry. You think I am crazy, don't you?" Chantelle is being honest. I reply with equal honesty, "No, I do not think you are crazy. What you are describing can happen to anyone, rich or poor, black or white. Life is about opportunities and choices. You chose to take drugs to help you cope. You are now an addict. There is a way out, an alternative way of coping. There are people who have beaten the habit. I can help you if you want me to?" She nods, "Another coffee?" she asks. I say yes.

Chantelle disappears into the kitchen; she returns five minutes later with coffee."There you are." She stands in front of the mirror, adjusting her hair. Her phone buzzes, a text message, "What time is it?" she asks."Eleven forty-five." I answer. Chantelle then disappears into the bedroom, calling out, "Sorry I have to get changed I am going shopping with a friend at twelve-thirty, is it cold out? Oh, never mind, can you just let yourself out. Bye."

I think I have just been dismissed. I take my cup through to the kitchen, rinse it in the sink, then I wipe the worktop where sugar has been spilled, there is a spoon on the windowsill with tiny white particles. I realise she has used cocaine despite my being there. Have I been talking to myself?

I call "Goodbye, see you tomorrow." Chantelle does not reply. I sit in my car outside and ring Chris I explain the morning events, he sounds positive, "At least she is talking to you, she recognises where she is at."

Then a taxi pulls up outside, Chantelle appears in what looks like an evening dress, with stilettos and gold wrap. She climbs into the taxi and is gone. Chris asks, "What has happened." I reply, "She has just left for work in full evening wear and on a high."

"Do not take it personally, you are doing well. Keep me informed."

**Tenth Visit**

I have visited Chantelle's flat every other day for over a week. Today will be my last visit. I have messaged her daily. Five days ago she replied saying she had gone to visit her father in Liverpool. We were unaware he was still in touch with her. There has been no further communication. I drive to the flat, it is raining again. I am surprised to see the front door is open, it has clearly been smashed open. I shout from the bottom of the stairs, Hello, is anyone there? Chantelle are you there?"

A male voice shouts, "Please wait, I am on my way." A smiling face appears on the stairs, it is Trevor the community police officer, "Hello Carla, what are you doing here?" he asks. "I am looking for Chantelle who lives here, I have been working with her. She has been out of touch for over a week." Trevor takes out his radio, he reports details of a break in at the address, a lot of damage. Owners whereabouts unknown. "Do you have a mobile number for her?" he asks. I give him Chantelle's number; Trevor informs me that I will have to go to the station and make a statement. "They will ask about the last date you saw her if she mentioned any plans. Details of any of her friends or contacts, so they can locate her.

It is a week later when I catch up with Chris, he has brought something to show me, it is a video on the internet. "We are supposed to be working" I laugh. Chris explains that someone messaged him a link to the video. We go into Bill's office. I am shocked to see on the screen the staircase leading to Chantelle's flat. There are several male voices, whispering, it is hard to tell what they are saying. Then the shot is inside the flat, Chantelle is there, she looks odd, she is struggling to speak. Then she is singing along to music, her body is moving seductively, there is clapping and jeering. The next shot shows Chantelle topless, still moving slowly, touching her body. She is not smiling, she looks like a puppet, her head is drooping to one side. She staggers, more shouting and jeering. It is difficult to tell how many people are watching. The next shot Chantelle is naked, I feel physically sick as I watch her, she is lifting her hair and closing her eyes, swaying. The clapping continues in a weird sort of rhythm. Suddenly she screams, a heart wrenching scream, I want to look away, I cannot watch her, yet I need to see. The camera turns away from her to someone's hand, he is holding a rat, a stuffed toy rat. The hand waves it in front of her, taunting, provoking. Chantelle screams and lashes out, her arms are thrashing around, as though there are a hundred rats attacking her body, she is frantic. The clapping and jeering reaches a crescendo then suddenly stops. Chantelle is on the floor, she is having a seizure. The filming stops. I am angry, I am disgusted, I am hurt for this violation of a young woman. Tears of frustration, I am unable to voice my feelings.

I look at Chris, we both stand in silence for several moments. Chris speaks quietly, "I have passed this information on to the police. I have checked with the hospitals in the local area and there is no record of Chantelle being admitted."

I want to cry but I am too angry, "Who are these evil bastards? Do the police know who they are? Where is she now?" I feel such an ache inside, "Do you think she is dead?" Chris shakes his head. "No, I am sure she will turn up. The police can trace the video, the phone and find those responsible." I stare at Chris, "Well I hope they throw the book at them!!"

**One month later**

Nothing has been reported in the press, no news reports. It is almost as though Chantelle never existed. I contact Trevor, he says 'off the record', Chantelle's case is not a priority, she is a known prostitute, a drug addict and has been in police custody several times. Her chaotic behaviour is well documented. Locally there have been two stabbings, a murder, several burglaries over the last month, including three with serious violence.

I write my last report on her file.

Life goes on, my case load has doubled, I too must carry on, more clients, more concerns.

One Wednesday I receive a call from the Northwest Regional Hospital Southport and Ormskirk. I am confused. "Hello, Carla Saxon Social Services how can I help?" I listen.

"I am ringing with regards to a Miss Longridge, she tells me you have worked with her." I immediately think someone wants a job reference. "Sorry, is this in connection with a job application?" The person on the other end of the line explains, "Sorry, I am Staff Nurse Susan Clayton, we have been treating this lady, she has given your name as a contact." I struggle, "Longridge, I am not sure about the name its does not ring any bells with me."

"Oh, well thank you, I suppose it's back to the drawing board, I will explain to Chantelle." Then the proverbial penny drops, "Chantelle, did she live in Sherwood Close?" The nurse gives an audible sigh, "Yes, yes that's correct." We discuss and confirm further details, date of birth, place of birth and father's name. "It is Chantelle, I know her as Redgrave, what has happened to her?" The nurse hesitates, "Do you know if she has any next of kin alive." I explain Chantelle's dysfunctional family.

The nurse informs me that Chantelle was taken to hospital over a month ago, she had jumped off the roof of an apartment block. She had been high on alcohol and drugs; it is believed she jumped to demonstrate she could fly.

"I am afraid Chantelle broke her spine; it is a serious injury. The injured spinal cord means the area is unable to send and receive messages from the brain to the body's systems. These systems control movement, there is a degree of paralysis. At this point we are unable to state how much, if any movement Chantelle will regain in her lower limbs. She will certainly be here for quite some time. I am sorry to have to tell you this over the telephone. I have been in touch with local social services, they are sending someone out next week. Chantelle was insistent that I ring you." I thank Staff Nurse Clayton and say I will get in touch with the social worker who has been allocated to work with Chantelle. I also promise to visit her on my next day off, which is Monday. I thank her for letting me know.

I am so pleased that Chantelle is alive, yet I am also incredibly sad that she has this horrific injury. I finish my shift. I am in emotional turmoil, yes, I am overwhelmed to learn she is still alive, how will she cope now? What will her future be? Chantelle will always be in my thoughts; I wish her nothing but health and happiness.

One choice, one decision and Chantelle's life could have taken a different path. Maybe now she will have another chance to find an alternative life.

# Chapter Five

# LILY

'Courage is what it takes to stand up and speak,

Courage is also what it takes to sit down and listen.'

Winston Churchill.

**First Visit**

Winter is probably the hardest time to work out in the community, with its cold dark mornings, scraping the frost off the car in the early hours, driving on icy roads through foggy patches. Standing on cold doorsteps trying to get a reply. Today is the first day of December and I am reluctant to get out of bed, it's warm and comfortable, Paul is asleep, why is it he never hears the alarm? I gently kiss his forehead, "Come on sleepy head, it's already seven thirty." Paul groans and pulls me closer. We cuddle for a few minutes; reluctantly I pull myself away and go for a shower. Today I am visiting a lady who lives in a remote area of the countryside, about five miles outside town. Her nephew rang and requested help for his aunt who is ninety- eight years old.

There has been snow overnight on the hills, here in the town the roads are clear. I wrap up warm, donning a thick sweater and trousers underneath my waterproof parka, I find my knitted hat and pull it down over my ears, then warm up the car engine. I will need my satellite navigation equipment, I am told the place is remote, the nephew Graham Strange, has given me directions. He said the road to the cottages is usually drivable, in the current weather conditions however, it is not really safe for cars. He has emailed me a hand drawn 'walkers map.'

It is nine thirty when I reach the car park, this is used mainly by ramblers and serious hikers, unseen from the main road, surrounded by trees. A small pathway is marked on the map Graham sent, I gather my bag and lock the car. Morning light is beginning to peep through the mist which hangs low on the surrounding hills and faint sunlight glistens on snow. I estimate the snow will reach the top of my ankle boots. I walk slowly down the icy path, it's only wide enough for one person, after five minutes I emerge on a single-track lane. There are fields to my left, I can see roof tops of the neighbouring village, nudging out from behind the trees. To the right is a stone wall. I turn left and walk up the hill, it is difficult to walk because the snow hides the ruts and stones of the lane, I feel icy wind biting on my cheeks.

After ten minutes, I see a row of cottages in the distance. The snow is deeper now, I have climbed considerably higher along the moorland lane, my trousers are wet, and the snow is sticking to the fabric, making them heavy. I wonder why I agreed to make this visit today of all days.

The cottages must be around two hundred years old, built in traditional dark stone, it looks as though there are three cottages in the row. From the lane I can only see the back of the cottages, the windows of the first one I pass are dirty, with jam jars and old boxes on the sills, they look like the windows of a garden shed, complete with cobwebs. The next two windows are boarded over. At last I arrive at the last cottage which seems to be the only one inhabited. Farm buildings, a barn and a lean-to shed housing a tractor, a chicken coop, and another low building lie across from the cottages, in a cobbled farmyard. Everything looks very picturesque in the snow and morning light. I stand and admire the view over the town for a few moments. Then I go to the first cottage and knock on the door.

The door is opened by a giant of a man, he is around sixty, with dark shoulder length hair and a bushy beard, which is greying at the edges. Dressed in many layers, with jumpers and waistcoat and a thick quilted jacket, he has wellington boots on, which I find odd indoor wear.

"Yes." He says gruffly, looking at me as though I have just interrupted a personal crisis. "Good morning, Carla Saxon. Social Services. I have come about Lily; we spoke on the telephone." He nods and steps to one side, indicating for me to go in.

Inside the cottage is spacious and untidy but warm. There is a log burner in the corner and the heat fills the room, a large oak table in the centre, is loaded with paperwork, plates, and the remains of a cooked breakfast. A small radio sits in one corner, radio 4 is on, it's a political debate. Graham stares at me, I realise I must look an odd sight, windswept, rosy cheeks and snow wrapped around my ankles like an additional pair of socks. "I didn't realise how bad the snow was. Or how far from the car park you are." I say as I take off my woollen hat, I am already too warm, my snow boots are starting to melt.

"I have been in to see Lily this morning and lit the fire, she always gets up early. She is a bit grumpy today, always finds something to complain about. Does not appreciate what I do. Not my responsibility you know. I have been looking after her since her daughter died. She can't get out, so I have to do everything, shopping, paying the bills, she thinks I should be at her beck and call twenty-four hours a day. I don't get paid for it you know, it's a bloody liability it is." Graham turns and switches the electric kettle on.

There are no female signs in the room, definitely a no-frills room. I ask, "Do you manage the farm?" "Yes, it is a bloody big responsibility, there are fifteen acres of land.. Most of it lies to the north and is out of use now. I can't run the place on my own; if she were not so bloody stubborn it would be sold by now. I am hoping you can recommend that Lily goes to live in one of those nursing homes, I have applied for Power of Attorney, her daughter had it, but she has gone now."

Graham does not look like a man who is over-worked, he is heavily set, his belly hangs over the top of his trousers. I am not sure how much to believe. "How long have you been caring for Lily." I ask. "Two months, she is hard work, rude too. I keep telling her if I go, she will be alone, no one else cares, she could die here, no one will know." There is a malicious tone in his voice, I wonder just how 'caring' this man actually is. Curious, I ask, "Does Lily live here with you?" "No, she is in the end Cottage, lived here for sixty-eight years. She was born on this farm, married a farm hand and moved into the cottage." He pours himself a cup of tea from the teapot. "I want some support for her, is there any financial help she could be getting? Help to pay for heating, things like that?" He drinks his tea. "There are financial benefits available, it depends upon circumstances. What assets the client has. Who owns the farm?" I am unable to give him a direct reply without more information. "She is the sole owner, don't know why she did not sell it years ago, bloody liability it is. The land could be sold off, instead of going to waste." Graham shakes his head.

"I think I should meet Lily now, is that alright." I turn towards the door. "Yes, go ahead. I try not to go in more than twice a day. Can you let me have the information about the money side?" He seems a little obsessed by money, I wonder if Lily has financial problems, "I will speak with Lily and come back if I have any queries."

The second cottage is boarded up. There is a cobbled path which links the three cottages, a small garden area lies in front of each one, with views over the surrounding hills. I can imagine it would be beautiful in summer, there is also something romantic about it now, the snow on the trees, conjuring up images of cosy log fires and old-fashioned Christmas celebrations. As I pass the window, I can see a faint glow inside, the windows are dark and dirty. The front door is wooden, it has not been painted for many years; a faded plaque reads 'Spring Cottage'. I knock on the door, on my third knock, I realise the door is not locked. I gently push it and walk in, calling "Hello, Mrs Cavendish, hello. Social Services." There is no reply. I find myself in a tiny sitting room, made even smaller, by the large bulky furniture. The room is very dark, especially having come in from the white landscape outside. A coal fire is lit in the grate, smoke is wafting into the room, I can feel it in my lungs already. There are soot marks above the fireplace, everything bears smoke stains from the fire, the windowsill has a coating of black soot. The chimney needs cleaning. There is an old-fashioned sofa in front of the fire, with a large overcoat folded on one side. The sofa has definitely seen many years' service, one of the armrests is missing and two books are wedged at one corner as support for a missing leg. The rug in front of the fire is dirty, threadbare with burn holes from ashes. I notice the rest of the floor is stone slabs, there are no other carpets. A large oak sideboard fills the back wall, there are various family photographs but the pictures are sepia and look old. My eyes are slowly starting to adjust and sting with the smoke, I see the walls also have streaks of soot. I call out again, "Hello, Mrs Cavendish are you there? Hello."

I walk towards a curtain which I assume conceals a doorway, I pull the heavy curtain to one side. "Hello" I shout even louder now. I am in a kitchen, another small room, it is the window onto the lane, the jam jars, boxes, blocking out any light. I see a small stone sink with a few dishes in. A cabinet, I remember the style from my childhood. We called it a kitchenette, a tall cupboard, this one is pale green with two top cupboards, which have obscure plastic panes in the doors. The middle piece drops down to form a shelf or working space with storage. There are two drawers and a two further cupboards at the bottom. As I daydream about this classic retro cupboard, Lily appears from behind another curtain, which conceals a staircase, leading to a bedroom. I later discover this staircase is unsafe, it is riddled with woodworm and there is a serious risk of someone going through it. I turn to Lily.

"Hello Mrs Cavendish, my name is Carla. I am from Social Services, did Graham tell you I was coming?" I wait for her reaction; she does not seem phased at finding a strange woman in her house. "Oh, I didn't realise that was today, I have only just got dressed, it is so cold." Lily picks up a small kettle, fills it with water then goes into the living room and places the kettle on the open fire. She indicates for me to take a seat, I sit in the armchair by the window, hoping to inhale less smoke from this position.
Lily returns to the kitchen, she comes back carrying a small plastic tray, with a tiny china teapot. Two odd, chipped china teacups and saucers, each stained from use. She places a non-matching milk jug and sugar bowl, on a small round stool.

The kettle is now seated on the glowing embers. I cough a little as some of the smoke hits my chest, my eyes are stinging, there is no air in the room. I ask, "Sorry Mrs Cavendish, do you prefer me to call you by your full name?" She replies, "Lily is fine by me." As she goes back to the kitchen, returning with half a packet of Rich Tea biscuits. She appears unaffected by the excessive smoke, I am still struggling, the more I try not to cough, the more I do.

"I am so sorry Lily, it's the smoke, your chimney needs sweeping." I cover my mouth with a tissue. "I've been telling him that for months, he just says, you show me the money and I will get a chimney sweep. I do not know why he thinks I have money; he takes my pension every week. He controls the purse strings. According to him we are paupers, penniless landowners." I watch Lily as she pokes the fire. She is small, I estimate around four foot eight. Of slight build, she could easily wear children's clothes. Her face bears the lines of many years spent outdoors, her skin is dark, her eyes are bright and deep blue. Her hair is tied at the back in a grey knot. Not a silver grey, a dark lustreless grey. I look up to see a thick cloud of smoke hanging on the ceiling. "I think I need to speak to Graham about the chimney, this is not good for your chest, all this smoke in the room." I watch Lily for a reaction, "He will not do anything, think he will be happy if I pop my clogs." Lily goes to the front door and she pulls it open. "Smoke will go in a minute or two." She mutters.

I need to assess how Lily copes with everyday living, so I start to ask questions. "How many rooms do you have in the cottage Lily?" She stares at me puzzled "What has that got to do with anything?" I smile, "As I explained to Graham, I have to do an assessment, detailing what care or help you may need around the home. I see you have a kitchen; do you have a cooker or microwave?" Lily tuts. "No, did have one a while ago but it broke, never used one of those new microwave things, don't trust them. Though I must say it is easier since Marjorie had the water connected, getting it from the well was a chore every morning." I need a few seconds to process what Lily is saying.

"So, you have nothing to cook with?" Lily shakes her head. "Who is Marjorie" I ask. "My daughter, she died you know, cancer took her, she was only sixty-two. Horrible thing cancer. Took my husband John too, thirty years ago." Lily is stoking the fire again. "Yes, it is, so sorry to hear that. Did Marjorie live with you then?" lily smiles, "No, Marjorie is married, or should I say, was married. They lived in the village. She used to come every day to see me. Must be five years since she got the water fitted, she was like a dog with a bone about it. Said she was sick of using the well. I have used that well all my life, did not do me any harm, fresh spring water." Lily sits back on the sofa.

I am amazed that Lily not only lives in a two-hundred-year-old cottage but has a lifestyle to reflect that era, there is no washing machine, no TV, no radio, no telephone. "Where is your bathroom?" Lily grins, "The lavatory is in the small building, over in the garden, to be honest, I have a commode in my room Marjorie got it for me, saves me having to go out in this weather." I am fascinated by Lily; she is very lucid; her conversation is lively and alert; she lives the life of a pauper. If what Graham says is true, she could sell the land and live comfortably.

"How do you get a hot meal?" I am expecting her to say Graham brings her food. "I can warm up soup, cook vegetables and meat on the fire. I manage a hot meal when I want one, cannot beat a baked potato cooked in the fire." The kettle starts to whistle, Lily removes it from the fire and fills the teapot.

I ask Lily if I can take a quick look around, she agrees and busies herself stirring the tea. I scan the 'kitchen' there is water but only cold. There is a large 'dolly tub,' I remember these. My grandmother had one for washing, it's basically a metal tub, which can be filled with water, you then need a posser, a wooden stick which has rounded forks at one end to churn the washing, a definite fore runner of the washing machine. I see a posser in the corner. There is another door, this one leads into the cottage next door, I peer inside, its pitch black, I remember the windows are boarded over. Not an ideal situation having empty boarded up rooms so close. I investigate behind the curtain and slowly climb the steep, narrow staircase, which creaks at every step. It opens into a small loft space, the eaves of the roof on either side. In the middle is a bed, there is little space for furniture. At the foot of the bed is a chest, presumably where Lily stores her clothes, a small commode is wedged in the corner. There is one tiny skylight, so dirty the light struggles to filter through.

After my short self-guided tour, I decide Lily probably would be better off selling up and moving. I thank her, say I am sorry, but I do not have time to stay for tea. I say goodbye, with a promise to be back soon to arrange some help. Outside I am glad to breathe in some fresh air. I return to the first cottage to speak to Graham.

Graham answers the door almost immediately, this time it is obvious that I am not to be invited in. His frame fills the doorway and he almost snarls, "What now?" I am a little taken aback by this aggression, "Erm, I believe Lily has asked that you arrange for the chimney to be swept?" He glares at me. "How am I supposed to pay for that?" I can see he is not really going to cooperate with this matter, "The house is full of smoke, it's unhealthy, Lily is inhaling all the smoke and soot, it really needs to be sorted." I am wondering whether to tell him I can probably get a grant to do it. "Not my problem, if she sold this place, she could live in luxury, she is just too stubborn." He moves to close the door.

"OK, well there are a few things I need to sort out for Lily, maybe I should just talk to her? Or would you like to know?" He hesitates for a second, "As long as it does not cost me money, do what you like." He then slams the door. Charming! I would really like to tell him exactly what I think of him, unfortunately, that will have to wait. I feel grumpy now, on the trek back through the snow, I plan all the modes of torture I would like to inflict on this horrid man, including stoning, needles in the eyes and hard labour.

By the time I get back to the office I feel much better. I make myself a cup of coffee to thaw out. My coat is hanging over a radiator to dry. I have to venture out to another appointment shortly. I finish my notes and make some enquiries. I arrange for a chimney sweep to visit the cottage as a matter of urgency, he will go the next day. I organise this through Age UK, who have vast resources and information available. They also offer to visit tomorrow, and I agree to meet their representative at the cottage, the lady says she will bring a selection of items, free to people in need. I then speak to another local charity 'Emmaus', originally set up to help homeless people. I know the manager. I explain I have an elderly lady in need of some furniture. I say that there is no money available to my knowledge, the client really needs a new sofa, not too large as it is a small cottage. Also, some form of rug, the bigger the better. I am not sure how Lily will react to this invasion, but I am determined to improve her situation. The manager says she will get back to me in a couple of days.

Bill has been in meetings all morning, he emerges just after lunch and calls me in. "Carla, I need a favour. What have you got on this afternoon?" I think quickly, "A one o'clock lunch call with Helen Smithers, a two o'clock visit with Ethel to the pharmacist to get her medication checked. So, I should be free by three. Why?" Bill smiles. "Great, I would like you to visit someone for me, to do an assessment. This man lives at home with his mother and brother, his mother has telephoned, asking for more support. She has approached the service requesting we find her son somewhere to live. It maybe we can just put support staff in to help on a daily basis." Bill passes me a form with the referral details on, "He is already on our system, please have a look at his information before you go. I think his mother can be a little difficult. Which is why I am asking you to go." Bill smiles. "Great, well I suppose I had a trial run this morning with a rude customer, what's one more between friends." I look at the form and leave.

I ring the number on the referral, for Mrs Hanlon. There is no reply but an answering machine, I leave a message, my name, telephone number and explain I would like to call at three o-clock today. I check out the file for Patrick Hanlon.

Patrick is forty-two years old; he lives at home with his mother and younger brother. His father died five years ago. Patrick is on the autistic spectrum and registered with the Learning Disability Team. His condition impacts his ability to interact with others and his communication skills. He has difficulty learning new skills and following simple instructions. Until five years ago, sole care of Patrick was undertaken by the family. Two years ago, he started to attend a day centre three days a week.

Patrick's mother is now sixty-four and feels unable to cope with his behaviour, she is struggling to meet his care needs. He apparently attends the day centre today until around four, which gives me time to chat with his mother, before I meet him. I jot down a couple of notes, before leaving.

I am running late on my calls, its ten minutes past three when I finally find the house, it is part of a complex one-way system, which means I go up and down the same dual carriageway twice. I hate being late. I press the doorbell, it is a nice part of town, other than its proximity to the busy road. I hear movement inside. Mrs Hanlon is a large lady, she has a round face, which would benefit from the occasional smile, her eyes are partly hidden behind thick rimmed glasses. I introduce myself. Mrs Hanlon looks me up and down then says, "You are late." There is a faint hint of an Irish accent."Yes, I am sorry, the traffic was very busy, I had to work out how to get to this road from the dual carriageway." I give a small smile. "You better come in then." She says as she turns and goes back inside, I duly follow.

We are in a long narrow hallway. On one side the wall is covered with pictures, photographs, oils and watercolours, there is barely an inch between each picture. The other side is just a line of coats hung on hooks the length of the wall, this makes the hallway appear dark and narrow. I follow her through a door on the right.

My eyes take a few seconds to adjust, I am on sensory overload. The room is L shaped, the rear set as a dining area. A stone fireplace runs half the length of the room, with a number of shelves inset. It is crammed full of ornaments and trinkets. The sort of things people buy at the seaside. Wall plaques with various sea views from around the North coast cover one area of wall, there are small vases, pottery seagulls, statuettes of various religious figures and painted icons hanging in the smaller niches. Silk and plastic flowers fill a variety of containers. Every flat surface in the room is filled, with what my late husband Martin called 'Stuff'. There is an enormous TV in one corner, a sofa and two armchairs, each laden with four or five pillows. I count four coffee tables, two standard lamps and two upholstered footstools. The window is adorned with large ornate glass figurines in various colours. I feel as though I am in a bargain basement Aladdin's cave.

Mrs Hanlon points to a chair, she sits in the other, which is clearly her seat, with knitting patterns, needles, plus assorted wool in bags by the side. "So, what can I tell you? Have you ever met Patrick?" I shake my head; I am busy getting out my notepad."No, I am looking forward to meeting him. How does he enjoy going to the day centre?" Mrs Hanlon clicks her teeth together,

"Patrick does not enjoy anything, he attends, he comes home, he does not talk about it. Not like my Peter, now he is a chatterbox. He has done well for himself Peter, got himself a good job, works for the Post Office, not a postman, he is in the office. Good looking boy my Peter. Never been any trouble, bright and popular, not like Patrick. He is slow, I think sometimes Peter got the brains for both of them. Had a lot of problems with Patrick, he went to a special school, where he seems to have learned little, except how to give me a headache. I cannot cope with him now, I am tired. His washing alone is too much for me." Mrs Hanlon gives a long sigh and adjusts her cardigan.

I find it difficult to concentrate with all the colours and clutter in the room. "What sort of things does Patrick need help with, is he able to prepare a simple meal?" Mrs Hanlon laughs and shakes her head as though I just asked her if her son can fly. I ask, "Can he make a drink for himself?" "He can get a glass of water but if you ask him to make a cup of tea, he will bring half a cup of weak dishwater. Then he leaves such a mess in the kitchen and spills everything, he is such a clumsy boy, leaves me the carnage to clean up. It is easier if I make it, or of course if Peter is home, he will bring us all a cuppa. Peter bought one of those fancy coffee machines, so I can have coffee with hazelnut or vanilla, such a thoughtful young man."

I scribble a few notes, I am now thinking Patrick will need a great deal of support. "What about Patrick's personal care?" Mrs Hanlon stares at me as though considering how best to answer, "Well, he can wash himself in the shower with supervision, Peter usually helps with that. He can clean his teeth but has to be reminded. I usually give him a shave. I select his clothes each day. I also have to change his pads, that is difficult for me now." Mrs Hanlon looks at the clock, "Patrick will be here any minute, the bus drops him at the door. Do you think you will be able to help?"

"I am not able to say yet until I have had a chance to meet Patrick. Does he have any physical disabilities?" Mrs Hanlon shakes her head, "No, unless you consider acute clumsiness a physical problem. He has no sense of value, money does not mean anything to him, he is not able to go out on his own, no road sense you see. Ah, there is the bus, please excuse me." Mrs Hanlon goes to the front door.

I listen to Patrick's arrival.

"Come on, hurry up, there is someone here to see you. Give me your bag. Patrick take your coat off, Patrick come here…" Patrick comes into the room, his coat half on, one sleeve trailing behind. He stops and gives me a big smile,

"Hello, I am Patrick. Have you come to see me?" Patrick is a forty-two-year-old man who has been dressed by his mother. His trousers are baggy and pulled up high above his waist. He is wearing an ill-matched red check shirt and a green striped tie; his anorak is bright yellow. His hair is short in a traditional cut, he has glasses. Before I can answer him Patrick asks, "Are you a social worker? I have Bob, he is my friend, he is a social worker. Is it my birthday? Bob always comes on my birthday. It's written in my diary." I form an instant liking to this chatty, amiable man.

"Now Patrick, go and hang your coat up and change your shoes then get your drink and come and sit down properly, go on, off you go." Mrs Hanlon stands waving Patrick out of the room. "He is such a daydream, I always give him a drink when he gets home, he is allowed two biscuits otherwise he ruins his supper." Mrs Hanlon sits back on the chair. Thirty seconds later Patrick appears with a glass of milk and two biscuits, he sits at the dining end of the room and quietly eats, keeping both eyes fixed on me.

Patrick gulps his milk down and almost runs back to sit next to me on the sofa. Mrs Hanlon clicks her teeth again, "Patrick, glass." He immediately jumps up and takes his glass and plate into the kitchen, returning to take his seat next to me.

"Do you work with Bob? Bob took me to the football match, do you like football?" Patrick is excited to have someone visit; he has a childlike enthusiasm. "Yes, I know Bob he works in a different office, he told me about you, he said you support Arsenal football team, is that right?" Patrick starts to fidget excitedly, "Yes, yes.

What is your name? Do you support Arsenal? Have you been to the day centre?" In the haste I forgot to introduce myself, I smile and offer Patrick my hand, "Good afternoon Patrick, my name is Carla, I am a Support Worker, I have not visited the day centre but I would like to. I am not really a big fan of football. What days do you go to the centre?" Patrick is still frantically shaking my hand; I gently pull it away. Patrick looks towards his mother, "When do I go to the centre mam?" she directs her reply to me. "Monday, Wednesday, and Friday. From nine until three- thirty." I look to Patrick, "Well Patrick maybe I can come and see you at the centre on Friday? What do you think?" Patrick begins to fidget with excitement. "Yes, yes, I will tell Denise that you are coming, I like Denise she helps me. Carla is a nice name, when is it your birthday Carla?"

I smile again with a genuine fondness for this likeable man, "Good, I will come to see you there. Now Patrick, what else do you like to do besides watch football?" Patrick stares to the wall, he is thinking. Mrs Hanlon speaks before he can answer. "He does not do anything, watches the TV with me most nights. Peter is always busy; he plays squash twice a week and he reads a lot. Peter sometimes takes Patrick out for a walk if the weather is good."

I feel I have enough information for now, I thank them both and agree to visit again with ideas for support, I will also visit the centre and arrange a meeting with Bob. I thank Mrs Hanlon for her time, Patrick insists on walking me to the door, "Nice to meet you Carla, if you tell me when your birthday is, I will put it in my diary." Patrick looks almost sad that I am leaving. "December third, my birthday, see you on Friday, Nice to meet you too." Mrs Hanlon calls out, "Patrick come on back in here now, let the lady go." With that Patrick turns and heads back, I close the door.

At five thirty I leave, I decided on fish for supper, so I need to call in the supermarket, picking up two pieces of salmon. I hope Paul likes salmon. As I walk to the cashier, I see tins of tuna on special offer, I decide to treat Mr Tom to some fish too. Paul rings he is going to be an hour late; he is stuck at the hospital with a client. I put some washing on and have a shower. We finally eat at nine, Paul's client was admitted following another seizure. He looks tired, and decides to stay the night, we are both asleep before ten -thirty.

**Second Visit**

There is still snow on the high ground but thankfully the main roads are clear. I trudge up the lane to the cottages, it's ten-thirty, I advised Graham yesterday that the chimney sweep would be there at nine. As I approach, I see a small van parked outside and a man is packing brushes away.

"Good morning, have you finished the chimney at Spring Cottage?" I ask. He does not look like a chimney sweep; he is wearing light blue overalls without a speck of dust. "Oh, yes hello. This lane is a little bit out of the way, need a four by four vehicle really. Took me half an hour to find the place." I nod. "Everything OK in the cottage?" I ask. He looks questioningly at me, "Yes, are you a relative?" I shake my head, "No sorry, I am from social services, I arranged for your visit." It was his turn to shake his head. "She should not be living like that, you people need to sort it out, that old lady needs to be in a care home. The house is disgusting. Who is that miserable guy who goes in? He is so bloody rude, I tell you felt like smacking him."

I understand his response, I have heard it before. Sometimes people just assume that social services have a magic wand, can instantly make everything alright. If only!

People have rights and feelings, if they want to stay in their home, if it can be done, ensuring their comfort and safety, then this is a better option. It is as important to listen to people's views as it is to act. I do not feel the need to explain anything to this man. I turn and walk towards the cottage. The door is open, I call hello and walk in. The room is like a fridge. Lily is in the kitchen tearing up some old newspapers. "Good morning Lily, are you alright? Do you need the fire lighting?" Lily turns and smiles, "What a nice young man. Graham has gone into town so I thought I would try and light the fire." The fireplace has been left tidy, I start to build up the fire with wood, paper, firelighters, and coal. After ten minutes we have a lovely glow. "Lily, I have arranged for a lady from Age UK to visit today, she is coming to talk to you about supplying a hot meal each day. I hope that's alright?" Lily holds both her hands out in front of the fire, "That's incredibly good of her, I do manage here you know, I do not eat much these days. Would you like a cup of tea?" I decline the cup of tea and offer to make Lily one, fetching the kettle from the kitchen. As we wait for the kettle to boil, I explain to her that I am hoping to replace her sofa and rug. Lily appears slightly confused by the offers of help.

Linda from Age UK arrives, she has walked up the lane from the car park and looks fresh faced from the wind. She is in her late twenties, dressed in many layers against the cold, it is difficult to assess her size. She sits down in the armchair and places her large bag on the floor in front of her. I introduce Lily.

She smiles, explains to Lily her role and opens her 'Mary Poppins' bag producing two light-weight thermal blankets, one which she wraps over Lily's legs. Also, two pairs of fluffy bed socks and a hot water bottle. There is a thermos flask, which Linda suggests will be useful to keep by her in the bedroom at night, or during the day to lessen the need to keep boiling the kettle. Next is a red woollen hat, gloves, and scarf set. Lily immediately tries on the hat and leaves it on for the duration of my stay. A packet of teabags, two packs of biscuits and a box of soup sachets, to make in a cup. Finally, there are two large blocks of milk chocolate, lily's eyes light up at the sight of the treats. Linda has arranged for a hot meal to be delivered every day at twelve o'clock, she describes some of the meals and the desserts provided, Lily's response is, "I will never eat all that food, you have already brought me so much. It feels like Christmas." Her eyes fill as she speaks.

Linda and I stay to chat for another thirty minutes. Lily tells us about the farm, eighty years ago, when she lived with her parents, her older brother and younger sister. Her parents and brother are dead now. Her younger sister lives in America. Marjorie, Lily's daughter, had contacted her sister Marigold, she now lives in a place called Palm Springs. Marigold is eighty-five now, Lily has not seen her since she had her twenty-first birthday. They keep in touch by letter and a few years ago Marjorie rang Marigold, they were able to chat for thirty minutes, Lily said this was amazing.
Linda and I say our goodbyes.

I promise to be in touch when I have news of the furniture. We walk carefully through the damp slush back to the car park. Linda asks," Lily appears to be in excellent health for her age, her hearing is good, what about her vision?" I agree with Linda. "Yes, Lily is great for her age, there is nothing on her medical records at all, in fact I think she is due a medical check-up, once we get things sorted. It is only the second day," I smile.

Back at the office I check my emails, one from Bill, inviting me to attend an interview for the post of Manager on the following Monday at ten. The interview is in the main council offices. I immediately feel apprehensive and doubts cross my mind. The brief says I need to prepare a short ten-minute presentation, about the merging of the two teams, the benefits and issues which might arise, along with suggestions for dealing with these. I decide to think about this later.

There is a short email from Paul, 'Hi, sorry I forgot to mention I am going to be at mine tonight, got washing to do…. a man's work is never done. Miss you already. xx Paul.

My friend from Emmaus Charity has rung me. I call her back, she has found a cottage style sofa, matching easy chairs, plus a foot stool. They can deliver on Friday morning between ten and eleven, I explain about the road conditions, she does not think there will be a problem. She also says there will be no cost, this has been cleared with the powers that be, because of lily's age and her circumstances. No one wants small cottage suites any more so there are plenty around. They will deliver free of charge but cannot remove the old stuff, especially as it does not sound salvageable. When Alan and Adrian come in later, I ask them if they can cover the visit on Friday, to take out the old furniture and rug. Also, to get the room ready for the new delivery, a sweep would probably be enough. Alan agrees but Adrian is busy, Shirley offers to go instead. I email Graham and inform him of the plans, I do not expect a reply.

**Third Visit**

Alan and Shirley leave the office early to prepare the cottage. I will go to the day centre at ten thirty to meet Patrick and the staff, I feel they will give me better insights into Patrick's abilities. The phone rings at nine forty-five, its Alan, "Just ringing to say thank you on behalf of Shirley and myself." I am confused. "Thank you for this lovely job, we have lifted the sofa between us, it has literally fallen to pieces. The bottom fell out. Do you have any idea how many creatures were living in that sofa? It is a wonder it did not bloody walk out itself. Shirley says she is traumatised by the number of beetles, spiders, earwigs, not to mention the dead mice, which fell out on the short journey to the front garden. The rug disintegrated so we swept that up. Shirley has just gone to ask the guy at number one if we can borrow a mop and bucket. We are then ready for the delivery. Lily is fine, she has put the kettle on the fire. Can't we get her an electric one?" I apologise, although I can tell Alan is laughing, I obviously had no idea about the true condition of the furniture. I say thank you and ask him to thank Shirley for me. They are so good, I am pleased to work with these two, nothing is too much trouble and they somehow always see the funny side.

The Day Centre is in a modern block, inside is a community centre, a public gym, a cafe, meeting rooms and on the first floor three conference rooms. The largest of which is used for the day centre. I climb the stairs, I can hear laughter, there is some sort of game taking place, everyone is obviously enjoying it. A large cheer rings through the stairwell, the game has been won. As I enter the room, I estimate there are about twenty people inside, a quick glance tells me the ages range from twenty to fifty years. I hear a loud "Hello" from the other side of the room and within seconds Patrick is by my side. He reaches forward to shake hands and is so excited, I am struggling to hear what he says. I am promptly rescued by a lady, who Patrick introduces as Denise.

"Wow that was a nice welcome." I say, gently recovering my hand from the vigorous handshake. "This is my friend, Carla. She is not a social worker and her birthday is in December." Patrick enthuses to Denise; I have never been introduced in quite this way before. Denise smiles and welcomes me. "We are just stopping for our mid-morning break; can I offer you a tea or coffee. "A cup of tea would be lovely, thank you Denise." "Milk and sugar?" I nod. "Patrick, can you please get Carla a cup of tea with milk and bring some sugar. We will sit over there by the window."Patrick nods enthusiastically and rushes over to a small kitchen area.

A few minutes later Patrick arrives with a hot cup of tea on a tray with milk and sugar. "Thank you, Patrick." Denise then asks him to join the others and have his coffee."Wow, that is a surprise," I am impressed by Patrick's abilities. "I was led to believe Patrick struggles to follow simple instructions, here he is making tea!!" Denise smiles, "When Patrick first came, he was frightened to do anything, he was convinced he would do it wrong, we have been trying to build his confidence. He is very able when here, but I am afraid he is not encouraged to do things at home." Denise offers me a biscuit. "So, do his family know how well he is doing?" Denise's expression is of frustration, she shakes her head, "No, I tried talking to Patrick's mother, she would not listen. I wanted to place Patrick on the independent travel programme, so he could learn to travel on public transport. She flatly refused. I suggested Patrick be allowed to use the kitchen more, we have regular baking sessions here and Patrick always participates. I feel with more support he could prepare basic meals for himself, Mrs Hanlon said absolutely not. Then I spoke to her about Patrick's toileting, did you know he still wears pads, adult nappies! Mrs Hanlon was incredibly angry when I raised this topic. She actually said we were only complaining because we did not want the task of changing him. She then kept him away for three weeks. Between you and me, we have been working with Patrick on this issue and he now goes most of the day without a pad, we put one on to keep the peace when it is time for him to go home."

Denise looks across the room to Patrick who is now preparing to participate in the Arts and Crafts session. He waves. "It looks like you have developed a good working relationship with Patrick. I did wonder about things at home. Do you know his brother Peter?" Denise smiles, "The golden boy you mean? Yes, I have met him once. In the last two years, Patrick has only mentioned going for a walk with Peter once, then without enthusiasm. Bob spends more time with Patrick, he takes him to the local football during the season, all in his own time of course.

I think because it is on a Saturday afternoon, Mrs Hanlon allows Patrick to go, so she can do her shopping."Patrick is now waving frantically at me, "I think I am being summoned to join him?" We both laugh, I join the group at the table.

This morning they each have a ceramic mug which they are decorating with bright coloured paints and stencils. Patrick is adding the letters PH, in red paint, the mug is white. He shows me a round stencil which he assures me is a football, his colours are red and white. The ball will be blue and white. I watch as Patrick lines up the letter stencils and tapes them in place. Many of the others around the table require a little more assistance. Across from Patrick is a young woman with Downs Syndrome, Patrick tells me her name is Louise. Louise is trying extremely hard to tape a stencil of flowers around her mug, but the shape of the mug is awkward. Patrick sees her struggle; he goes around the table and shows her how to do it. It is still not straight. However, Louise is happy because Patrick has at least managed to stick the tape down. I chat to Patrick during the session, he is relaxed and cheerful. He likes to ask questions too, "Where do you live? Do you have children? When are their birthdays?"

At the end of the session I feel I have a completely different picture of Patrick; I am convinced that Patrick will do much more if he is away from his mother, living independently with staff support. I do not feel her behaviour is purposefully designed to harm or deskill him. However, unwittingly she appears to be holding him back. Sometimes caring too much, being over-protective, especially when a child has special needs, is too easy. Now Patrick is older, Mrs Hanlon is struggling to care for him, she has raised her concerns and requested help.

I say goodbye to the group, many of them insist on giving me a hug. Patrick produces his diary to show me his newest addition, he has added my birthday in December. I say goodbye to the staff and Denise whispers, "I hope you can help Patrick; he has a lot of skills to offer." I smile and say, "I will give it my best shot."

Alan and Shirley are in the office between visits. They are both in high spirits enthusing about their day. Shirley in particular shares her experience with me. "I could not believe that sofa! The state of it. When we got the stuff outside the place looked bare. I borrowed a mop and bucket, drove to the nearest shop, bought some nice smelling disinfectant, then I gave the floor a once over. How did they manage in the old days with those stone floors?" Alan is smiling, Shirley always gives one hundred and ten percent. Alan confirms that the charity delivered a smart two-seater cottage suite, two armchairs and a footstool. When they had left Lily had been sitting in front of a lovely fire, feet up on the footstool, warm blanket around her legs and a thermos of hot soup by her side. "She looked a picture." Alan said with a smile. "Did the rug arrive?" I ask. "Rug? More like a fitted carpet, we had to lift the legs of the sideboard to fit it in."

I finish my assessment of Patrick Hanlon and though I have not been asked, I add my suggested action plan, then forward the email to Bill. It has been a productive day, busy but enjoyable. I have one more visit then I am finished for the day. My last call is to a man of eighty-three, he had just been sent home from hospital this afternoon. I am going to make sure he has everything he needs, some food for his supper, his medication, and a warm drink. His son will visit later in the evening.

When I arrive at Henry Dowson's home, he answers the door after my first knock. He struggles to walk, he has a walking stick, but he is obviously in some discomfort as he manoeuvres around the doorway. I help him back to his chair. "Good afternoon Mr Dowson, I hear you have been in hospital. How are you feeling now?"He is leaning back in his armchair, his face is contorted with pain as he moves, " It's Henry love, I have had better days. I am glad to be home though, do not like hospitals, they are full of sick people." He gives me a mischievous smile. "How about a nice cup of tea?" I ask. He grins and says, "That will do nicely, black two sugars." I go into the kitchen, which is simple, clean, and tidy. I soon discover the tea and sugar. I check out a carrier bag on the worktop, it contains a loaf of bread, a pack of ham, some eggs, bacon. milk and cereals. This has obviously been left by a family member. I make the tea.

"So, Henry are you hungry? "I ask. "Aye love, I have not eaten since seven o clock this morning. Been waiting around for the transport to bring me home. It is like Bedlam up there. They are waiting for your bed. Almost as soon as I got up, they had it stripped and ready for the next, sent me and my bags to the visitor's lounge, to wait for my lift. I am starving." I smile, he reminds me of my grandfather. always smiling even when the chips are down. "In that case, how about I make you a ham sandwich to be going on with? I know your son is coming around later with some hot food for you." He nods, "That'll do just fine lass." There is something heart -warming about being called lass, especially when you have passed forty.

Whilst Henry enjoys his sandwich, I ask him where he keeps his medication. "There is some in the top right-hand cupboard and there is a carrier bag somewhere I brought back from the hospital. I go into the kitchen, the cupboard is a miniature pharmacy, there are boxes and bottles of medication. I take down a few, some of these are out of date by as much as five years, technically useless. Others have labels worn away, so the date and dosage is indecipherable. The entire cabinet needs to be sorted and unwanted medication taken to the Chemist. I look around and find a large NHS carrier bag on the chair, this contains a wash-bag, two pairs of pyjamas, half a bottle of cordial and a packet of chocolate biscuits.

There is another bag which I remove and take into the living room, this is the medication. I empty the bag onto the sofa, there is an assortment of tablets, some boxed, some in foil packets and some in a white envelope? I have no idea what any of it is for, the ones without packets have no dosage, the boxed ones appear to be different variations of the same medication. The ones in the envelope are a complete mystery.

"Henry, these are all mixed up, do you know which tablets you take?" Henry looks at me and grins, "Eh Lass, they changed my pills that many times I don't know if I am coming or going." I am worried because usually there is a prescription sheet, listing the medication. I decide to ring the hospital, after several minutes of being transferred from one department to the next, I finally speak to the pharmacist. When I explain the problem, she is first in denial, then she is horrified. Medication should not leave the hospital, without correct packaging and labelling. The tablets in an envelope are definitely a disciplinary offence.

After a long conversation, in which she agrees to reissue the medication correctly, I agree to return the current medication as it was sent, I will also email her exact details, this I will do tomorrow morning. The pharmacist has Henry's details on the computer, I can collect the new medication in one hour. I sit and chat to Henry, tidy the kitchen, sort out his belongings from the carrier bag and make him a second cup of tea. I then head for the hospital in rush hour traffic. I collect the medication and return it to Henry.

When I arrive Henry's son is there, Henry has explained what happened. "This is disgusting, I do not think my father was ready to come home so soon, it was just they wanted the beds. It's a good job you sorted the medication because I would have been furious, bloody incompetence." I can see the son will not let the incident go, I explain that I would be placing a full complaint the following morning. In defence of the hospital I suggest they were probably rushed off their feet, maybe a trainee nurse had been asked to put Henry's things together? I did agree it was totally unacceptable.

It is eight thirty when I open my front door, Mr Tom has given up on me and is asleep on the sofa. I do not feel like cooking. I make myself some cheese on toast and a cup of tea. I take a shower, then climb into bed. Someone is going to get into a lot of trouble tomorrow, it does not sit easily with me. I text good night to Paul and my head hits the pillow for instant sleep.

The entire weekend is spent preparing for my interview, Paul is very patient, he listens to my presentation and offers constructive criticism, my biggest problem is saying too much. Paul says, "You cannot tell them their job, just put forward ideas. You have got to leave them something to do." By Sunday afternoon we have both had enough, we take Paul's dog Brutus out for a long walk in the countryside then stop at a pub for supper.

**Fourth Visit**

It is another cold morning, thankfully there is no snow, however, plenty of black ice, which is worse for driving. I arrive at the office early and start to draft an email to the hospital, I have been given the email address of the pharmacist and hospital CEO. It is self-explanatory, so once finished I forward it to Bill for approval. Some days it feels as though problems are always knocking at my door.

At nine-thirty I head off to my interview, my presentation on my lap-top, I want to look as professional as possible.

When I am called in, they are running fifteen minutes late, I read this as a bad omen, maybe the presentation before mine was exceptional? I see the person leaving, I recognise her, she smiles, "Hello," as she leaves, she manages a team in the sheltered housing section, strong competition. The interview is chaired by Brian, head of service, Bill is sat next to him, on the other side is a young woman from HR. They do the formal introductions, then each ask me questions from my CV. The woman from HR is Hilary, she has bright red hair and freckles, I estimate she is in her early thirties, trying to make an impression."Carla, I see you spent many years in HR, how do you feel that will influence your role as a line manager?" Good question I think, just wish I had more time to prepare my answer. Instead I waffle on about man-management techniques and employment law. I stop myself because Bill is shuffling papers, which he always does when he is getting bored.

I am then invited to talk through my presentation, I can see I have scored points by having it on my laptop, with charts, actions points, pros, and cons. I spent several years as a training manager; presentations do not phase me. Afterwards they thank me for my professional presentation, they will be notifying the successful candidate next week. When I leave, I feel full of confidence, by the time I reach the office I have analysed every aspect of the interview, I am now convinced I completely messed it up.

I contact Bob Collins, the social worker involved with Patrick, I want to arrange a meeting to identify options. I have worked with Bob in the past, he is an old friend, the sort of friend who will always listen, never complain, always offer sensible, no nonsense advice. Bob is ex-army; he was a sergeant and served in Eastern Europe and Northern Ireland. He would frequently keep everyone laughing, with tales of army life, the pranks he pulled with his colleagues. Bob is full of fun. Every Christmas he dresses up as Santa Claus and does charity visits to the children's ward and the local hospice. He is football mad, which explains why he takes Patrick to the matches. Bob says he will be near the office later today so can look in and see me, we agree to meet at three o'clock.

The walk to the cottages seems even longer today, with cold blasts from the east wind in my face. My ears and nose are freezing. I go directly to see Lily, there is smoke billowing from the chimney which means Graham has been to light her fire. As I pass the first cottage the door opens, Graham calls out to me, "Did you manage to get the information about financial help?" He is rubbing his hands together to ward off the cold and stands back for me to enter. I walk into the warm living room and reply, "I have spoken with the finance people, to apply for financial aid we must first do a financial assessment." Graham looks frustrated, "What do you mean, all Lily has is her pension, what else can they assess? Just bloody red tape, a person could starve to death waiting for bureaucracy." I try to tactfully explain,

"They have to investigate any other sources of income and assets, the fact that Lily owns the property will be taken into consideration. They will need access to Bank accounts, current and savings accounts and details of all assets. They will also look at weekly expenditure and cost of living expenses. It's a complex procedure, with a lot of boxes to be ticked before anyone is awarded a government grant." Graham walks across the kitchen area, and slams his fist down on the counter, he his breathing heavily. I look around, part of me is planning my escape route, I make towards the door, "So, you see it is a complex process." Graham shakes his head in disbelief.

"So, when can you do this?" I am quite relieved to tell him it is not my job, "Oh, I do not do the financial assessment, that is completed by the finance department, they will be in touch with you later this week." I smile, as I leave, continuing down the path to Lily's cottage.

I have arrived later, so I can be here when her first hot meal is delivered just in case there are any issues. I knock and Lily calls for me to come in. Lily is sitting on her new sofa with her blanket around her knees, Linda's gifts are certainly being utilised I smile, "Good morning Lily, how are you today?" Lily looks up, she is holding a large magnifying glass to read yesterday's newspaper, "Cannot see so well these days, never much good news in this paper." She places the tabloid on the sofa, "Come sit down, would you like a cup of tea?" I decline the offer of tea; Lily already had the kettle on the embers.

"Lily, Alan who came yesterday has suggested you might like an electric kettle; I can organise one for you, if you would like?" Lily stokes the embers as she replies, "I had one of those, Graham said it was broke, so he threw it away. It was a nice white kettle; I could see how much water was in it and it switched itself off when the water boiled." I smile, "OK, I will sort that for you." Lily starts to make herself a thermos of tea. I explain that the people will deliver a hot meal at twelve, I ask her if she has eaten breakfast, Lily points to the packet of biscuits on the stool. "Does Graham not bring you breakfast Lily?" I am remembering the remains of eggs and bacon in his cottage.

"No, he says he does not do cooking, he comes in and makes up the fire every morning though." Lily places the thermos on the stool for later. "I have lived here since I was born you know, lived with my parents until I was twenty. Then I married John, he had worked on the farm since he was fifteen. He always had a soft spot for me, he was just five years older, would have been one hundred and three this year!" Lily adjusts her blanket and continues, "We had Marjorie, she was the apple of his eye. Did well at school, she was very bright, went to University you know. Studied finance and business law, she did well for herself. She married Douglas, a banker, so they were very comfortably off, not short of a few shillings."

I am now curious about Marjorie. "So, Marjorie lived locally then? Is her husband still living?" I ask. "When they first met, they were at university in London, they had a flat together there. Then they married and bought a house in Brighton. They did not move back here until they both took early retirement, must be about ten years ago. Bought a nice house in the next village, used to be the Manor house, lovely old property, I remember it from when I was a child. Douglas died a year after they moved here, heart attack. Marjorie was devastated, poor lass. They never had any children."

I see the sadness in Lily's eyes as she remembers her daughter. "That is so sad Lily, good thing she had you, you must have been a comfort to her" Lily nodded, "It was a blessing having her around, she was a good girl, wanted me to move in that big rambling house with her, never stopped trying to convince me." Lily stared into the fire; it is difficult to believe this lady is ninety-eight years old.

"I would imagine Marjorie just wanted you to be comfortable, it cannot have been easy living in this tiny cottage all those years." Lily looks up, surprised, "No my dear, I lived at number one, I only moved in here when Graham arrived. He realised there was a serious problem with the roof at number one, the beams had rotted you see. It was not safe for me to live there. He got some quotes from various builders; it is going to cost over five thousand pounds to put it right. Graham sorted it all for me and helped me move my stuff in here. This place had been unoccupied for nearly twenty years. The builders have been paid half the money. They cannot start work until next year, after the bad weather. I am so grateful Graham was able to sort things out."

I have a strong sense of unease; something is not right. "When did Graham arrive here?" I ask. "Oh, let me see. Must have been about ten days after Marjorie's funeral, her friend Alison came and took me to the service." Lily pauses, I can see the memory is upsetting for her. "So, Graham is your nephew, is he Marigold's son?" I need more information.

"Yes, yes he was raised in America but moved back here a few years ago. The strange thing was she never told me she had a son, I always thought because she was a spinster, never married, too ambitious, children were not in her plans. Marigold owned a chain of stores in America, selling cosmetics, she sold the business for a small fortune about twenty years ago. Graham said he was the result of a short love affair Marigold had with a married man, illegitimate was the word he used. He said

Marigold had been a good mother, though he always felt he was 'in the way' of her business. It was so fortunate he turned up here. I felt so sorry for him, I think Marigold was very cruel to him, just judging by some of the things he has told me. Are you sure you do not want a cup of tea?"

Before I can reply there is a sharp knock on the door and a male voice calls,
"Hello, am I at the right address, is there a young lady by the name of Lily living here?"
A jovial man in his thirties comes in, he is smiling and winks at Lily as he says, "Oh, you must be the lady in need of my delicious a la carte menu, do you have a plate?"Lily smiles, I go into the kitchen, he follows me. Together we sort a plate, some cutlery, and a tray, which he carries back into Lily. "There we are madam, I hope you enjoy, chicken roasted to perfection with potatoes, green beans and gravy. With my delicious trifle for dessert. I will return tomorrow with some more deluxe cuisine to tempt you. Thank you and Good day." With that he leaves.
Lily grins, "Oh to be fifty years younger," she laughs, "Wouldn't mind him leaving his slippers under my bed." Lily giggles at the surprised look on my face. I decide to let Lily to enjoy her lunch. "I must go now, there will be another visitor at tea-time, to help if you need anything." She is already tucking into the chicken dinner, nods, and waves. "Bye."

I tap on Graham's door to let him know Lily has received her lunch, he calls out for me to enter. I notice on the table, a white, electric kettle. "Is that Lily's kettle?" I ask. Graham is startled for a second, "What? Oh, yes, it's broke can't be fixed." I also note two blocks of chocolate on the table. Graham follows my gaze, "Lily does not eat sweet stuff, she is border-line diabetic." I smile and thank him, there is nothing on record to say

Lily is diabetic. I grab a sandwich on the way back.

After lunch Bob arrives and we retreat into one of the interview rooms to discuss Patrick. Bob has known Patrick for over ten years but only been his allocated social worker for the last three years. It was Bob who persuaded Doris, (Mrs Hanlon, apparently Bob is on first name terms now) to allow Patrick to attend the day centre. Bob describes Patrick's first day, "I took him on the first day, he chatted in the car on the way there, once we went through the main door he froze. He actually looked terrified. I think I realised then the Patrick has never been socialised, he was not familiar with public places, or other adults, he had led a completely sheltered and isolated life. Other than school, he was completely isolated from the world around him. Denise has been brilliant; she has helped him with his confidence and his social skills. They take the group out once a month to activities, Patrick has been to the library, bowling, shows and art galleries. Last month they went to the Science and Industry Museum in town. He really is capable of much more."

I can see Bob is very keen to make Patrick's life better. "I hear you take him to the football too?" Bob nods, "yes, I am not sure if he fully understands the game, but he seems to enjoy it."

I continue, "Well, I suppose the question is what can we do to improve Patrick's life?" I am sure Bob has been considering this question for a long time. "I have put Patrick's name down for a place in 'supported living accommodation'. I already work with clients living in the house I have in mind. It would be ideal for him, there are spaces for two males and two females. I have a feeling a space may be available soon. I will keep you posted. I think Doris is genuinely struggling to cope now, Patrick can present challenging behaviour sometimes." I am surprised to hear Bob say this, I ask "In what way? Patrick appeared very calm and polite when I met him." Bob shakes his head, "Mostly at home, he can have tantrums, like a naughty child. I have only seen it once, I think there is a lot of rivalry between the two bothers and Doris fuels the situation, always taking Peter's word. Doris says when Patrick gets really upset, he will hit his head against the wall, he apparently did this frequently as a child; had to wear a helmet for his own protection. I suspect most of it is frustration, Doris still treats him as though he is five years old. Since he has been attending the centre, he has become less tolerant of Doris and Peter and has started to answer back and to sulk."

We both agree Patrick needs to move out as soon as possible, I ask Bob if there is anything I can do. Bob suggests I write a report of my findings for Patrick's file, to support the move into residential care. I agree, there is little else I can do at this point.

This evening I decide I need a little time to pamper myself, I put on a face pack, give myself a manicure and generally unwind in front of the TV. My daughter rings, to ask if there is news of my job. We chat for almost an hour, she is so like me it is scary, we laugh and get angry at the same things. After the call I think of her childhood, I too tried to do my best, just as Mrs Hanlon had. Unfortunately, Amanda grew up at a time when my health was at its worst. She would go to school in the morning and return home to find I was in hospital, she would sometimes go to bed, to awake next morning to find her Grandmother preparing breakfast. There was so much uncertainty, so much stress for a young mind.

When she was eight years old, I became ill on holiday, I

spent a week in a Turkish hospital. We travelled back to the airport in an ambulance, I was in a wheelchair. We knew it was my heart. The only other wheelchair passenger was a young man, we waited to be boarded first. His leg was in plaster, "What happened to you?" I asked. "Crashed my scooter, went over a wall. What about you?" I casually replied "Oh, I crashed when I was paragliding." His face was a picture. I thought it was more interesting than,' I have heart disease.' When we got back my health deteriorated, within weeks I knew I was extremely ill.

One morning I was feeling so ill, I asked Martin to phone for the doctor. When he arrived, he ordered an ambulance. I was then whisked away to the local accident and emergency department. I heard chatter as I lay waiting in the emergency room, "Yes, heart disease, been to Turkey, left lung has collapsed, in complete heart failure". Next a young doctor was by my side "Carla, you are very poorly, we are going to put you to sleep for a little while to get you better, is that alright?" I remember nodding, at that point I did not care what they did.

Amanda would next see me on a ventilator, with numerous tubes going into my body, I was in an induced coma. The prognosis was not good, they said there was only a fifty percent I would survive. Martin brought her daily to see me, she read me stories or drew pictures with the nurses. It was not easy for either of them.

I was completely unaware of anything, other than a feeling that someone kept on hitting me hard on my chest and back. I did not understand until later, it was the physios encouraging my lungs to clear and start working again. I had vivid hallucinations, I waved to the man in the bed opposite, (there was no bed or man) I watched as numerous Chinese people wandered by and appeared to be shopping. My mouth felt dry. I asked a nurse what time it was, I realised, I was in a hospital ward. The nurse advised it was five o'clock in the morning, on Christmas Eve, I had been in a coma for six days.

I left hospital fourteen days after my arrival, weighing just over six and a half stone, feeling incredibly weak but extremely grateful to be alive and able to tell the tale. Unfortunately, it was not a cure, my illness continued for many years. Amanda not only had to cope with my ill health but also her father's cancer and death. For a long time after my coma, in every family picture, Amanda drew me, with wires protruding from all parts of my body. I remember her being curious about my catheter, I explained to her what it was, she thought about this then said, "mum, you lose all your dignity in hospital don't you." Such a mature comment from a nine-year old!

I feel pretty morbid. I climb into bed, my phone rings - it's Paul, he too wants to know how the interview went. I tell him OK. I do not want to guess the outcome. He is confident the job offer will come. We say goodnight and agree to meet for a quick bite tomorrow lunchtime.

I review my interview again and remember when I went to work at Heathrow. I wanted to work at the airport, there were plenty of opportunities and the pay was good. I had been made redundant from my previous job. I joined the airport duty free staff. I will never underestimate the skills needed to do that job again. We worked in seventeen different currencies, had complex electronic tills to operate, worked long shifts, in a continuously busy environment. We were paid just above the minimum wage. The difficulty was that many people would pay for their shopping in more than one currency, sometimes paying with four or five, each time the exchange rate had to be re-calculated and the price adjusted. To add to the drama, we were allowed to be ten pounds over on the till takings, however, if one of the cashiers was five pounds under, then the entire team would lose their weekly bonus. I lasted six weeks.

By then I had applied for another position in the airport. I wrote to the senior manager of the duty free and advised him of their shortcomings. I then joined the Airport Authority, as a security guard. Following a two-week training course, I was working on the terminals. I loved the work - different people, different situations.

Seven weeks later, a job advertisement was posted on the internal noticeboard, for a security training officer. This was my dream job, I had trained for this, I decided to apply. I had to apply through my line manager, he laughed in my face "You have only been here two minutes what the hell do you think you know about the job. There are people with twenty years' service applying." I was embarrassed but determined, "Am I not allowed to apply then?" He threw an application form across the desk. "You want to waste your time, carry on."

I applied. I got an interview. The entire staff were anti my application, "Who does she think she is? What makes her think she can do the job? I think it is rigged, why else would she get an interview?" All the negativity made me uncomfortable but determined.

I bought an expensive suit for the interview and had my hair styled, confidence I decided, was the key to success. I had just completed the training, so the knowledge was fresh in my mind. I was proud of my efforts at the interview. A week later I receive a call, "Carla, we will be offering you the job. However, you should know that a representation has been made by the Trade Unions. Until you have completed your probationary period, technically, we cannot offer you the job. So, we will confirm your appointment in two weeks' time, together with a start date of the first of the month. Congratulations." Of course, it meant I had to suffer two more weeks of sarcasm and insults, no one was actually sure who had got the job, no announcement had been made. Slowly the reject letters started to arrive. People began to speculate who had been appointed, which made work more awkward.

It took me five weeks to change the negative attitudes into respect and I did that purely by accident. Ironically, I achieved this by dismissing a new recruit, stating that he had not reached the required standard. Inadvertently, I had somehow raised the status of a security guard.

I yawn, my eyes close. Another day.

**Fifth Visit**

I ask Bill if I can have a word. I explain my concerns about Lily and Graham, I tell him how Graham just appeared, how Lily had no idea about him, about his obsession with money, about Lily's sister in Palm Springs. I tell him about the builder and the five thousand pounds, I even tell him about the kettle and the bars of chocolate. Bill listens intently then says, "so what do you want to do?" I know what I would like to do but that would definitely be overstepping the mark. "Is there any way we can first of all check if Graham is who he says he is? Then maybe we can find out what he has done with Lily's five thousand pounds, surely this will be a police matter then?" Bill chews the end of his pen, he is thinking, "We do not want to frighten him off, so if you are right, we need to be sure of our facts. Do you think Lily will have an address for her sister?" I say, "I am not sure, I can ask. However, Graham has moved all Lily's things from number one cottage to number three, so you can bet your life he destroyed any evidence." Bill stands up, "I will have a ride up there with you this morning, we will see what we can find out, if you are right Lily is in the hands of an extremely hard, ruthless man."

When we finally arrive at the cottage Bill is panting, "Bloody hell Carla have you been walking up here every visit?" I laugh, "Bill you are out of condition, we have all been walking up here, through the snow too!" Lily is in her usual position near the fire, I introduce Bill and we sit down. Lily offers a cup of tea and Bill is horrified to see her place the kettle on the open fire. He starts to chat to Lily about her family, the past, her brother, and her sister. He carefully extracts the information he needs without asking direct questions. "It's supposed to be a very nice part of the world Palm Springs, do you know exactly where Marigold stays, near the beach maybe?" Lily cannot remember, she gets up and pulls a small shoe box from the sideboard, she passes him a letter addressed to Marjorie, it is from Marigold, Bill looks at it and passes the letter to me. He then engages Lily in a conversation about three photos which she says are her parents, her husband, and her sister when she was ten years old.

Whilst they chatter, I take a note of the address it is dated eighteen months ago, so I hope the address is valid. Bill is fascinated by Lily; he is laughing as she openly flirts with him.

Bill offers to put the box away for Lily, just as he sits down the door opens and Graham enters. "Bloody Hell, takes two of you to visit one old lady now does it? No wonder the council never has any money." Bill stands up, "Have we been introduced? I am Carla's manager; I always visit staff at their place of work, it is part of their supervision. You are?" Graham is obviously unhappy about our presence. "Who I am is none of your business. Until the council can provide some financial assistance for this lady, I am using my money to support her. You lot need to get your fucking act together." I can see Bill is fuming he stands and looks Graham in the eye, "Excuse me, I would appreciate it if you would not use such language in the presence of ladies. We will not be bullied as a service; your Aunt will receive everything she is entitled to as soon as the paperwork can be completed. In the meantime, my staff have done everything in their power to ensure her comfort and well-being. I will be making recommendations for this matter to be finalised at the earliest opportunity, when I get back to the office." Graham looks at me and then at Bill, "Well just make sure you do, my Aunt is very frail and needs care and financial security." With that Graham leaves the cottage. Lily is quiet the entire time Graham is here, "He is very highly strung, not a family trait. I think he worries too much." Lily whispers just in case he is loitering outside.

We say thank you to Lily for her time and goodbye, with a promise to be in touch soon, we set off back to the car. "I do not trust that man." I say as I sit in the car. "No, I think you are right, first thing we must do is get a number for that address, it's a Rest Home, so it should be easy.

Back in the office, I find the number and dial, It rings a couple of times then a young woman answers. "Hello, who is calling please?" I explain who I am and that I wish to speak with Marigold, the voice asks me to hold. A click later, a lady's voice with an American accent answers, "Sorry my dear I was just finishing my round of afternoon Bridge. What is this about?" I explain that I am working with Lily, she asks how she is doing, I explain she is well. Then I say, "May I ask you a question, do you have a son?" Marigold goes quiet, "Why do you ask?" I try to explain, "We are looking into Lily's living relatives for her records, to keep next of kin details." I do not want to be too direct. "No. I do not have a son. I do not have any children." Now please tell me the real reason you ask; I decide to be honest and explain the Graham situation, without sounding too accusatory. Marigold listens.

"I thought we had seen the back of him. Marjorie rang me about two years before she died and asked me the same question, he had visited her with the same story, a very astute young woman Marjorie. He still managed to extract over a thousand pounds off her, saying he needed to fly back home to America to visit me, said I was losing my marbles! The cheek of it! He had been staying with her for a couple of weeks, she had been giving him free board and lodging. Can you believe that? I do not think she had fully recovered from the death of her husband; she was extremely vulnerable. I know we have not been a close family; however, I hate to think of this imposter taking advantage. He must have done a lot of research; he appears to have known a great deal about me. Which I personally find very frightening. After our phone call Marjorie threatened him with the police, she sent him away with a flea in his ear. I think she was embarrassed by the entire incident; she did say to me he was very convincing. I think you are dealing with an extremely dangerous conman." Marigold sounds genuinely concerned.

I thank Marigold and tell her we will be contacting the police immediately, as we believe he has been obtaining money through deception, he is an imposter who is seeking financial gain. I assure her that I will take care of Lily. I ask if I might give her details and number to the police she agrees. Bill is in a meeting, while I wait, I write a report on the telephone conversation, I need to be careful and record everything.

We have a staff meeting scheduled at two o'clock, I had arranged to meet Alan and Paul at twelve thirty to grab a bite to eat before the meeting. It does not look as though Bill will be back for some time, I leave a note for him to call me.

I suppose I am seeking a little moral support as, we have not heard who has got the manager's job. Paul and Alan arrive together, just as I take a seat with my coffee and sandwich. Alan has been with Arthur Smethurst, he has been supporting him weekly, for over three months. Arthur lives alone in a sheltered housing scheme; about ten minutes away from the centre of town. The bungalows are for the over sixty-fives. Many of the bungalows have been adapted for wheelchair access. Arthur is active, for his eighty-five years, he regularly goes to the gym for a morning swim, he plays bowls every week with the local team and once a week he attends a tea dance where he leads the ladies in the sequence dances.

I wave, "Sorry did not get you two anything. I was not sure what you wanted."They return from the counter with a coffee, sandwich, and fudge cake, this is unusual, as Sylvia keeps Alan on a strict sugar free diet. He sits down,
"What a morning, been at the doctors with Arthur for the last couple of hours." He sips his coffee, "I arrived at nine as usual, knocked on the door, no reply, I tried a few times but still no reply. I looked through the living room window, no Arthur but the TV is on full blast, Arthur never watches TV in the morning. I

walk around the bungalow, no sign of him, his bed is made. In the kitchen everything is neat and tidy. I try the living room window again then tap on the glass. I was sure I heard a groaning sound. Last week he agreed for a key safe to be fitted, its scheduled for delivery tomorrow. I contact the Lifeline team; I know Arthur has a personal alarm in the event of an emergency. They have not heard from him but sent staff out with a key. While I am waiting, I look through the window again, I could just see Arthur's foot behind the sofa, he was on the floor. I rang an ambulance."

I am now fearing the worst, "Is he alright?" I ask. Alan continued, "I thought he had suffered a stroke or something, he is so fit, it was scary seeing him there. When we got in, he was conscious. the two young ladies from Lifeline managed to move the sofa and check him over. He had leaned over to unplug his lamp, lost his balance and fallen between the wall and the sofa. He was wedged and could not move. We estimated he had been lying there for at least fourteen hours, he was stiff, he struggled to move both his legs. He is alright now, the paramedic checked him over and advised him to see his doctor, for a check-up. I think he has given himself a shock, he must have been scared, stuck there all night. I took him to the doctors. He has a clean bill of health and is now wearing his wrist alarm. A bit late, however, I have a feeling he will wear it all the time in future. Now, have you heard any news yet?"

I smile and shake my head, "Nothing, so no news is good news maybe?" We chat for a few more minutes then head back. When we arrive, the main office is full, there are no seats, everyone is here for the meeting.

When Bill arrives, I head for his office, I explain what

Marigold has told me, he immediately rings the Police Station. Bill knows many of the officers there, he speaks with the duty sergeant, who passes him on to the fraud officer. Bill outlines the situation with Lily and confirms that she may be in danger. "Graham, or whatever his real name is an aggressive man, we believe he may already have taken five thousand pounds, if not more from Lily's account." The police arrange an appointment for us to visit the station at two o'clock this afternoon. Bill and I will attend, so the team meeting will need to be cancelled, it is rescheduled for the following week, amid lots of moans and groans about full dairies and important meetings.

At the Police Station we are taken into an Interview room and given coffee. Chief Superintendent Alex Mellor and Police Constable Anna Bridges come into the room, the chief superintendent knows Bill, they exchange a couple of pleasantries about family and golf. Then he asks me to explain what my concerns are with as much detail as possible. I try to keep to the facts, Lily's age, her family situation, her home, what details we have of her financial situation. I confirm that Lily is healthy for her age and has no memory issues that I am aware of. I describe Graham, without using the word imposter, his apparent knowledge of the family, Marjorie, and Marigold. I express my concern about the level of neglect and isolation Lily has experienced. I describe my understanding of the money Graham has taken for 'Building work' from Lily in addition to having full control of her bank account. I also mention the money he obtained from Marjorie before she died. We share information about Marigold, confirmed that Graham has been living there since Marjorie's funeral which was six months ago. I even mention the kettle and chocolate, though it sounded quite petty in the bigger scheme of things. PC Bridges has made copious notes and requested clarification on some of the issues. It is two hours later when we leave the station. A police visit will take place later that evening, they request that Bill and I attend, to be with Lily, whilst they interview Graham.

I will visit Lily at five o'clock, the usual teatime visit, the police will arrive fifteen minutes later. Bill says he will also accompany me, which I am grateful for, we do not know how Graham will react.

Later as we walk to the cottages it is already dark, this is the first evening call I have made, I realise how scary it is for staff to walk up this lane alone, I am grateful Bill is with me. He reiterates what I am thinking, "We may need to look at two staff on the evening calls." The lights are all on in the first cottage. Lily has a small reading lamp on, and I realise there is no main light in her living room. The fire at least is warm and welcoming. Bill and I debated in the car whether Lily should be informed of what is happening, we decided to wait until after the police have been.

We have arranged a temporary place of safety for Lily in a sheltered housing scheme, which I will take her to later. If she is willing. This entire situation will be very upsetting for her.

Lily as always is welcoming, her first thought is to offer tea, which Bill accepts. I proceed to make her a sandwich for her supper, I also make up soup in her flask for later. From the kitchen window I see two police vehicles arrive and four officers. Bill is chatting about the cold spell and Lily was reminding him of the winter in nineteen seventy-six, which was far worse.

We hear the hammering on the door and raised voices, Lily looks at me, her hearing is perfect she knows something is happening, "What's going on?" Lily asks. Bill explains, "It's the police Lily, they have come to talk to Graham, he may have been a naughty boy." Lily looks at Bill accusingly, "A naughty boy, I am ninety-eight years old do not treat me like a child. Why are the police here?" Bill explained that Graham may not be who he says he is, that Marigold never had a son." Lily reflects upon this for a few moments then says, "I think I knew there was something odd about him, he does not look like any member of my family, we have extraordinarily strong genes, you know. He has been helpful though, making my fire, buying my shopping, paying my bills.

That is assuming he has actually paid them?" Lily gets up to stoke the fire, "So, is there a problem with the roof?" Lily looks to me now. "I doubt it, I think he wanted your property. Marjorie met him, he tried to take money from her, but she realised and sent him away." Lily looks a little shocked by this. He knew Marjorie?"

We hear raised voices from number one, the sound travels through the cottages, which are all linked internally. Lily says the cottages had been one big farmhouse originally, her parents had divided it into three, when the children grew up. There is shouting and swearing now, we can hear Graham's voice. There follows a scuffle, the sound of furniture being overturned. After a few moments it goes quiet, we listen, almost afraid to breathe, sitting quietly staring at the fire.

A loud rap on the door and we all jump. PC Bridges calls out. "Police, may we come in." Before we can reply they are in the room, the other policeman with her is introduced as PC Quinn.

Lily, Bill, and I learn Graham is not his name, he is

known to the Police in London and Scotland for fraud. His real name is Frank Bowden. Although he has several pseudo names. He was born in Doncaster, although, he has lived in various parts of the United Kingdom, he has never been to America, in fact he has never been abroad.

Apparently, he is very gifted with computers and had created several fake identities for himself. He had served eight years in prison for property fraud in London, obtaining mortgages on properties, under false names and renting them out. The police will now take various documentation from the cottage to be checked. Initially, it appears Frank has applied for a secured loan, using Lily's property as security, for a large amount of money. There are no builders engaged to undertake work at the property. Frank, (Graham) fails to co-operate with the police, he resists arrest, during a struggle he assaults a police officer and threatens other officers with a knife. He is now in custody and will not be coming back for a long time.

After the police leave Lily looks calm, I wonder if it is delayed shock. I ask her if she will let us help for a couple of days, we have a place where she can stay, to give her the opportunity to consider what has happened. I then take her into number one cottage where a call is made to Marigold. They talk for thirty minutes, I return to cottage number three and go upstairs to pack a bag, I am hoping Marigold can convince Lily to come with us, if only for a couple of nights. As I climb the rickety staircase my foot goes through the rotted timber, fortunately, I have a strong grip on the rail, I still graze the skin off my right shin. This makes me even more determined that Lily should not spend another night here. The police are returning to the first cottage in the morning, to check for evidence, so Lily cannot stay there. Thankfully, when Lily finishes her call, she is more than happy to leave the place for a few nights and is even considering a trip to America.

By nine-thirty she is sitting in a small, clean, centrally heated apartment with its own kitchen and bathroom. She is looking somewhat shell-shocked, so many things, so many changes it is a lot for anyone to deal with. I stay with Lily until ten thirty, then the staff bring her a cup of cocoa and say they will sit with her, until she wants to sleep.

I look at my phone, five messages from Paul, he must be worried, in all the excitement of the day, my personal life has been placed on a back burner. I forgot to let him know I would be late. He is at my house. I message just to say sorry; I am on my way. It is almost eleven when I get home, Paul is not happy. "The least you could have done was message me, I have been sitting here all evening imagining the worst." I apologise again, I explain its been frantic today, I just forgot. This enrages him even further "Just forgot? Is that what this relationship is? You can just forget I exist?" I look at him, he is very angry, I have never seen this side of him, I am tired, "Sorry Paul but this was a big case for me today, I have had a stressful day and I am very tired. I really don't need this now." Paul stares at me, his face is flushed, he grabs his jacket and heads for the door. "OK, if that's the way you want to play it, have a good life." He pulls on the door, "Paul don't be silly, you are over-reacting, let's have a drink." Paul turns to me "No thanks, see you around." With that he is gone.

Mr Tom brushes against my leg, almost on cue. "Hello, little man, I imagine you have not been fed yet?" I go into the kitchen and fill his bowl. I am not hungry; I realise I have not eaten since lunchtime. I make a cup of tea and a banana sandwich, which I force myself to eat. Then I shower and climb into bed. The sleep fairy is on strike.

**Sixth Visit - Times are Changing**

It has been over a week since Lily moved into the apartment block, staff report that she is to settling in, she repeats the story of Frank (alias Graham) to anyone who will listen. Lily and Marigold have agreed to keep in touch and ring each other more often.

Today the full team is in the office, I suspect Bill is planning to tell everyone about the proposed amalgamation of the two teams. He calls me into his office. "Carla, I plan to talk about merging the two teams this afternoon. I am also going to introduce the new manager, if she doesn't mind it being done this way." I watch him, he has just the faintest hint of a smile. "What do you think, is this afternoon a good opportunity to tell everyone you got the job?" I am stunned, pleased, nervous and a little scared. The overall feeling, however, is one of satisfaction.

Lacey is in the office today, looking radiant after a two-week holiday to the Canary Isles. She is sporting a golden tan and a newly cut and permed hairstyle. Her attire is less flamboyant than usual, a thick quilted, full length overcoat. Underneath, she reveals her true colours with a blue denim dress, adorned with bright yellow sunflowers, added at random to the fabric, she has high boots and a scarf which if unravelled will stretch the entire length of the room. Lacey unloads a box of biscuits onto the table, "Mrs Dudley has sent these in for the team to say thank you for all your support." Everyone is thrilled by the gesture; a little recognition goes a long way. Lacey asks me if I can spare an hour at ten o'clock to attend a visit with her, I feel since our last disastrous visit together, when we went to the wrong house and offered support to the wrong person, Lacey is eager to show me she does really know what she is doing. I agree to go.

We climb into Lacey's car which is again full of rubbish, despite the fact that she has not used it for two weeks. There is a definite smell of rotted food. She explains. "We are going to the flats in the north of town, you know the ones behind the swimming pool?" I nod absently. "The guy's name is Robert Finlay, he is twenty- five and has just come out of prison. He served eighteen months, of a three-year sentence for burglary, prior to this he has been in court for joy-riding, underage drinking and shoplifting. He has no contact with his family, his father is in prison and his mother still lives in town but refuses to have him in the home, he apparently stole from her and ransacked her home. Robert also spent some time in Borstal following his involvement in drug related crime. I am already imagining a cocky youth, who knows all the answers - lazy, smoking pot, all the stereo-typical images of a young thug.

When we arrive at the first floor flat, Robert answers the door, he is tall, clean shaven wearing a tee-shirt and jeans. He still bears the look of a young boy but there is a sort of deep sadness about him. Lacey explains who we are, he invites us in. In the living area he sits on the sofa, "I was just trying to tidy up." He says looking at me. I look around the room, "Have you had burglars?" I ask. Robert shakes his head look of despair.

The room is in chaos, there are papers all over the floor, cupboards have been emptied, there are empty lager cans everywhere. He shakes his head, "No, these are my 'so called' mates. They found out the prison had arranged this flat for me and they all decided to visit last night." Robert puts his head in his hands, I can see how upset he is. Lacey asks "So did they do this damage? Why on earth would you let them in? You know you could end up back in prison?" Robert looks up, there are genuine tears in his eyes, "there were six of them, what am I supposed to do, they just came in, ate all my food, wrecked the place. They brought drugs in. I am clean, not touched anything in over a year. I hate this!" Robert is now crying, there is something that I find really upsetting seeing a young man like this in tears. Lacey appears unaffected, "How did they know you were here Robert; did you tell someone? How could they know, you have been out of prison for less than twenty-four hours?" Robert looks through his tears, wiping his eyes on his sleeve. "I did not tell anyone. They went to my mother's house, the bitch, she told them where I was. I hate this, I really hate this. I wish I were back inside. I was safe there; I knew what I was doing. I was happy there." Robert begins to cry again, I dig out a tissue and pass it to him.

We help to straighten the flat, Lacey arranges for new locks to be fitted, we both know the 'mates' will be back, the locks will be no deterrent, Robert is terrified. Lacey asks if I will accompany Robert to the supermarket to replenish his cupboard, he has no money, the little cash he had, has been taken. Lacey arranges for a small amount to be provided from petty cash, she hands Robert twenty pounds from her own purse. He insists on going alone to the local mini market,saying he needs to clear his head. Lacey and I stay to finish tidying the flat."This is a really difficult situation, what can we do? I ask, "They will obviously be back; he is so vulnerable." I feel that whatever we do will not be enough. After an hour Robert has not returned. We go to the mini market and inquire if anyone has seen him. The shop manager informs us that Robert has just been taken to the police station, he was caught shoplifting. "Strange really, he actually took three bars of chocolate from the shelf and looked in the camera before heading out of the door, almost like he wanted to be caught."The shopkeeper explains. Lacey heads off to speak to the police, I return to the office.

It is almost time for the Team Meeting, I feel so low after the morning visit. I have no idea what the outcome will be. Alan and Shirley come in together, they are both smiling. Alan has been to see Arthur, who has now found himself a new lady friend "and she is only seventy-eight" Arthur had enthused, Alan is laughing. Shirley has been to see Lily, who is very content in her new temporary home, so much so, she has decided to stay there and sell the farm. She wants to leave most of her monies to animal welfare charities, although she is planning a trip to visit her sister in America. Shirley laughs, "I wonder if she would like a personal chaperone? I am free." It is great to hear some positive news.

The meeting is full, all the cases are given a mini review, an update so we all know what is going on. Lily has secured a place in the residential home; a family solicitor is handling the sale of the property. Graham's (Franks) court case is scheduled for next month. Bob tells us that, Patrick has now been offered a place in the supported living house and will move in next week. The list seems endless, some sad outcomes and some good.

Bill explains about the amalgamation of the two teams, no one seems surprised, rumours are rife in the organisation, everyone has a theory. There is a question and answer session, Bill is able to supply all the answers. There will be one team it will be larger than the current team, initially it will be increased by ten new staff, other staff will be redeployed, in other areas of the service. Our team will remain intact unless anyone has a specific desire to move? After this Bill announces that as of the first of January the team will be located in new offices on the old industrial estate, at the South-west part of town. The new office space will be larger, with additional computers, better storage, and a bigger coffee machine. A loud cheer rings out. The new manager will be Carla Saxon. The room goes quiet for what I feel is an eternity, then Alan says "Well Done! Carla." Everyone claps and someone shouts speech. When the clapping stops and silence resumes, I say, "Thank you all so much, I am incredibly pleased to continue working with you all. As always it is a team effort. We are going to undergo a few changes and probably have a bigger, wider clientele but it will be interesting and a great challenge. Thank you for your continued support. Oh, and by the way, who is selling the tickets for our Christmas party?"

# ABOUT THE AUTHOR

Carole Parker grew up in Greater Manchester, when she was twenty-one years old, she moved to the South of England. Her career has taken her from the cotton mills of Lancashire to the executive offices of Heathrow.

Carole returned to Northern England in 1989, where she opened and managed her own retail business. In 2002 she received a heart transplant and returned to work in 2003. In 2016 Carole decided to move to the Greek island of Syros. Here she purchased a traditional farmhouse in need of renovation. She now spends her time working on house projects, writing, painting and looking after an ever increasing number of stray cats.

Carole spent ten years employed in social care, working in the community. It is from this experience she wrote the books '**Who Cares?**' and '**Someone to Care**'. However, all the characters and situations are fictional and not portrayals of any real clients she encountered.

Carole's next book '**Put it Down to Experience**', is scheduled for release in November 2020. This book is a 'tongue in cheek', humorous look at life through the eyes of a forty-something, single, female.

# "Put it Down to Experience"

'A selection of stories from the life of a forty-something, single, woman.'

## By Carole Parker

# Due for release November 2020

# The Almost Hijack

'I'm not afraid of storms for I am learning how to steer my own ship'

Louisa May Alcott

**All Aboard**

The warm air hits me as soon as I step out of the plane, I cannot believe I am here. I struggle down the steep steps and trundle my compact case across the tarmac to the Airport building, the sign says, 'Welcome to Turkey', I feel another quiver of excitement. It is not my first trip here, I have visited on three other occasions, it is my first visit as a single, forty-something woman. We are quickly ushered through the passport control and directed to a further counter to pay our entry visa.

In the Arrivals Hall I scan the sea of faces holding name cards, I have paid for transfers from the airport to the port of Marmaris. Then I spot him, a small slightly overweight man, with a black moustache which covers half his face, he is waving frantically at another single woman traveller. His card definitely has my name on it 'Ms Cathy Sidebottom', not the most attractive name for a possible romantic adventuress I know. The woman waves him away; he is searching each new face coming through the gate. I go over and tap him on the shoulder, "Ah Gunaydin, Ms Cathy? You travel with 'Mavi Gokler' the cruise?" I do not speak Turkish, however, I do have odd words, so I wish him "Gunaydin" which is good morning. I then say, "Blue Skies Cruise?" in English with a Turkish accent. I can tell he is impressed with my command of the language.

"This way please." He grabs my case and sets off at a gallop across the hall towards the door. Once in the taxi I begin to have doubts, what if there is more than one Blue Skies Cruise? I decide to get confirmation by explaining I am travelling with the 'Sophisticated Singles Cruise Holiday Company'. "Doldurulmus ispanakla seyahat ediyorm", I say in my best Turkish. He turns and stares at me, I feel extremely uncomfortable, he is travelling at a speed of fifty kilometres on a busy road, without looking. He shakes his head and turns the radio up, so now any conversation is drowned by Turkish music. I re-consult my beginners guide to Turkish, slight error in translation, I have actually said, "I am travelling with stuffed spinach."

This is my first time I have been on a 'cruise' singles holiday.

`We arrive at the port, there are so many Gulets docked I wonder how I will find the right one. My Driver knows exactly where to go, he weaves through the crowd and comes to a halt in front an impressive, polished wooden gulet. The words 'Blue Skies Cruises' are waving from a small flag. The gulet bigger than I expected, it is approximately twenty- five metres long, with two masts and an engine, it is capable of sail or power. The brochure says there are eight individual cabins, a kitchen, Crew quarters, a communal rest area, two sun decks, large dining area. There will be a crew of five plus the captain.

The driver unceremoniously drops my case on the ground and stands staring at me, I am wondering if he thinks I have to pay? I prepaid with the cruise, I hand him my voucher and pick up my case. A wooden bridge connects the ship to the dock. The driver calls out, "Ingiliz koylu ipucu yok." I turn and wave, "Thank you, Bye." He repeats this time he is shouting "Ingiliz koylu ipucu yok! I turn and give him my final wave. A handsome young man is there to help me and my case over the short bridge, "Welcome to Blue Skies, you are Miss Cathy?" I nod and smile, thinking to myself, how can I possibly wear a bikini if the crew all look this good.

"You forget to give driver a tip maybe?" I feel my face flush, "Oh, sorry, yes I forgot." He smiles to reveal a perfect set of white teeth, "No problem, we are used to English miss-understanding. My name is Yusuf, I am one of the crew. We have one other guest arrive, I can introduce you, this is Annie, from?" The blonde woman smiles, "Annie from Newcastle, welcome aboard" Yusuf turns to me, "Can I get you something drink, wine, beer?" I see Annie is drinking a bottle of water, so I ask for the same.

The deck is much wider than I imagined, with wooden seats built into the structure, all covered with bright cushions in vivid colours. It is almost lunchtime here, the sun is high in the sky I have been warned about the sun. I am not one of those people who develop into a bronzed goddess after a few days, I tend to look more like a chameleon, mid-colour change, with red, orange, white patches and the odd scales where I peel. I imagine Annie will bronze easily. Yusuf brings me a bottle of water and disappears below deck. "So, Cathy, where are you from and why did you decide on this cruise?" Annie leans back into the cushions and drinks her water. "I am from Manchester, I am not sure why I picked this cruise, I suppose I just wanted to put some adventure into my life. I am a widow, it is this first time I have travelled abroad alone." Annie sits up and whispers conspiratorially. "The rooms are not that good, ridiculously small and nowhere to put clothes. The Crew are really fit though! So, I suppose there is some compensation." I smile, "well I suppose they have to be fit, working at sea every day, steering this, it reminds be of a traditional galleon, like the pirates used to have." Annie sinks back into the cushion and takes another sip of water, "Well, I hope the other passengers are good looking, or I might just have to get to know the Cook a little better, have you seen him, he is delicious, Omer, even his name sounds sexy don't you think?" I watch Annie as she drains her bottle, "Well I suppose so, it's a bit like Omar Sharif, he was quite a lady's man I believe." Annie looks puzzled, "Who?" I explain he was a famous actor, "starred in Funny Girl and Doctor Zhivago." Annie appears to be losing interest, "Oh, wasn't Johnny Depp in the Dr film too?" I shake my head, "I doubt it." Annie stands, the boat sways a little, probably more so when one is standing. "Just going to sort my case, be back in a few minutes." Annie disappears down below deck. I have no wish to miss the glorious sunshine by being below deck, I lean back and close my eyes. This is just what I need, relaxation, peace, sunshine.

I waken to the sound of English male voices, Yusuf is welcoming three men aboard, Yusuf does and excellent job of remembering and pronouncing the names, "This is Cathy from Manchester." They all smile and nod, the older one stands forward and shakes my hand, "Nice to meet you." Yusuf continues, "Cathy, this is Charles, from London?" he looks for confirmation and Charles nods. Charles looks to be in his fifties, maybe older. He is tall, with a dark, slightly receding hairline, his sunglasses conceal his eyes. He is wearing a cotton shirt with bright patterns of tropical plants, a heavy gold bracelet and knee length shorts. I notice something shining around his neck, oh no, he is a medallion man! I have always been wary of men with excessive showy jewellery, as I find they frequently have a personality to match. "This is Matthew, from Brighton I believe?" Matthew nods. I estimate Matthew's age at around forty- five, he has a nice face, nice in a non-descriptive, boring way. He smiles and I feel there is an open honesty about him.    "And this is Keith from Birmingham," Keith smiles and offers me his hand. I think to myself; Annie is going to be sorely disappointed with this selection. However, on the bright side it may be the Cooks lucky day. Keith is slender, whiter than his white tee-shirt, fair haired. He looks anxious, maybe he is just overwrought from the journey. Yusuf explains that we are still awaiting three more guest, who are arriving in the next hour. Olive also from London, Maddie from Scotland, and Kaylee from Essex.

A quick calculation tells me there are three men and four women, the cruise was advertised, 'Definitely not a dating cruise, this is an adult cruise for friendship, conversation and shared adventures, exploring the sun-kissed Mediterranean, in a traditional Gulet Cruise ship.' So, I suppose it does not matter that the men are out- numbered, I am sure they will not mind in the least.

The men all opt for beer. Annie returns now wearing a skimpy bikini, sunglasses, she is carrying a packet of cigarettes and a fresh bottle of water. Yusuf introduces her to everyone. If she is disappointed in the male selection, she does not show it. If anything, Annie is chatty and flirty, laughing a little too loudly at Charles joke, tapping his shoulder and giggling at the punchline. Charles encouraged by this produces several more droll one liners. Annie eventually asks him what he does for a living, "I am a JP, a Justice of the Peace." Annie is suitably impressed, "Like a Judge you mean, sitting in court?" Charles does not bother to correct her, just nods and smiles.  Matthew is now sitting beside me; he is incredibly quiet. "Have you visited Turkey before I ask. "No, Although I have travelled quite a bit, mostly when I was younger. Always wanted to visit Turkey, it has a great history you know."  I agree, "I have been before and have visited many of the historical sites," he is extremely interested and I chat about Ephesus and Aspendos.  I ask him what he does for a living, he replies, "I am a Grief Counsellor, working with a local hospice." I think this must be the most depressing job on the planet, he is probably going to be a bundle of fun to holiday with." That sounds a difficult role, hard to console people when they lose someone." Matthew sits up straight, "The Lord helps me. I am a priest."  I try to hide my surprise, he does not look like a priest, no robes or collar, in fact he is wearing a tee shirt, shorts and sandals. I gaze at him, maybe a little too long. I muse, he could be a priest, maybe he is an undercover priest man. I smile at my own private joke.

Keith and Charles are now deep in conversation, I only hear snippets, but it sounds as though Keith is trying to sell Charles Life Insurance. I later learn this is Keith's profession. He asks if I'm fully covered.  Do I worry how my family will manage financially if anything happened to me?  "Are you aware of the average cost a funeral is these days?" he asks. I shake my head, "No I cannot say it's a subject I ponder on, is this your first trip to

Turkey?" I try to redirect the conversation. "No, most people do not think about it, a human failing, death is one of the inevitabilities of life," he smiles. "I have been coming to Turkey for the last ten years, with my girlfriend. We broke up six weeks ago." Keith is staring into his beer; I offer my words of wisdom. "Oh, I am sorry to hear that, it is always difficult when a relationship ends. You are probably doing the best thing; a good holiday will be a fresh start for you." Keith looks at me, "It was very humiliating, she left me for another woman. I had no idea. We had booked this cruise together, then she tells me out of the blue, I am bored of Turkey, bored of you, I am going to Skegness with Emma." Keith gazes out to sea, I wonder if he is contemplating suicide by drowning. I am relieved that Annie has now come over to join us, "Would either of you like a drink, they have just brought some cold beer and wine up?" Keith volunteers to fetch the drinks. Annie whispers in my ear, "Certainly no eye candy on the male guest list, looks like I will be giving the cook his oats later." Annie smiles and winks at me, I am still unsure how serious she is.

Yusuf appears and explains, "the others are on their way, when they arrive, we intend to sail to a nearby island where we will dock for the night. There will be time for a quick swim before supper, which will be served at seven." Annie is now reclined across the cushions, with her arm draped over the back, behind Keith's head. Keith looks uncomfortable and slides along a little way.

Kaylee arrives in full style, she has three cases, one large, one medium and one which she later explains holds her essential creams. Kaylee is larger than life, tall, attractive, and confident. Kaylee is definitely an Essex girl. Yusuf cannot do enough for her; he immediately finds her a glass of cold white wine, then struggles down the stairs with her three cases. It is difficult to assess Kaylee's age, I learn there is only a few months between us, she appears much younger, confident and slimmer. Despite this I find I like Kaylee, she has a wonderful smile and her self-confidence is refreshing. She asks me," Do you have anything to read, I have brought three books, I am happy to share." I admit, "I only brought one book, a thriller." Kaylee smiles and winks, "I am reading the Virginia Monologues, I will lend it you." I have never heard of it; I wonder if it is some form of advisory medical book.

Olive and Maddie arrive in the same taxi, apparently Olive, having lost her bag in the airport, missed her transfer. Fortunately, she had bumped into Maddie, they were both seeking a taxi to the port. Olive hardly speaks to anyone for the first hour. Her answers are yes or no, eventually we all run out of ideas and conversation starters, so Olive is left in peace to observe. Olive is extremely skinny, I guess she must be a size six. Thank goodness for Olive and Keith, there are now at least two people whiter than me. Olive does eventually speak, she asks, "Do you know where the toilets are?" I direct her to the ones on deck, explaining there are more below deck. When she returns her cheeks have a little more colour, she smiles timidly, "Seasick, I do not travel well." I wonder how she can possibly be seasick when we have not yet left the harbour?

Maddie is a little grumpy, she had been delayed by one hour at Edinburgh airport, they did not have her favourite perfume on the plane and they mixed up her pre- ordered meal, attempting to give her chicken when she is a vegetarian. The cabins are like small cells, she feels claustrophobic in hers. She has forgotten her hair dryer and there isn't one in the room. Despite having what she describes as her worst day ever, Maddie looks smart, tanned, her hair is neatly permed into soft curls, her manicure and matching pedicure neatly painted in soft peach. I do wonder if the tan is from of a bottle. Maddie has a long conversation with Annie, in which Annie explains, "I am divorced, I thought we were happy, I trusted Dave, I never so much as looked at another man. That is why it is so hard to take, when I discovered what the bastard had done, I wanted blood, his blood. He suddenly declared one day he was leaving, moving in with Julie, Julie the bloody Avon Lady. Julie who never got my order right! Julie who suffers from acne, Julie who already has three children! Dave always said he hated kids! I spent a fortune with her, and this is how she repays me. I would not mind so much but the bitch never delivered my last order, which I had already paid for! "Annie is reclining on the seating as she divulges her innermost feelings, none of us realise that the water she is sipping, is slowly plaiting her legs. Maddie, a stoical kind of person, listens to Annie then philosophically offers words of comfort and advice, "Shit happens. You just have to get on with life."

November 2020